"You need not be a deserted bride."

Shelagh drew her hand over her brows. She must be dreaming, for Cesare's proposition was utterly fantastic. Not many people seemed to bother about family honor nowadays.

And yet, he had offered to marry her in his son's stead.

The idea was enormously attractive. It would preclude the necessity of returning to London to face her friends' pity and contempt—contempt because she had allowed herself to be so easily beguiled.

But was it a good enough reason for a loveless marriage with a man old enough to be her father? A man who was practically a stranger—and an intimidating one at that!

OTHER
Harlequin Romances
by ELIZABETH ASHTON

1421—PARISIAN ADVENTURE
1453—THE BENEVOLENT DESPOT
1534—COUSIN MARK
1636—FLUTTER OF WHITE WINGS
1659—A PARADE OF PEACOCKS
1713—ALPINE RHAPSODY
1741—MOORLAND MAGIC
1762—SIGH NO MORE
1786—ERRANT BRIDE
1810—THE ROCKS OF ARACHENZA
1835—DARK ANGEL
1853—THE ROAD TO THE BORDER
1869—THE HOUSE OF THE EAGLES
1891—SCORCHED WINGS
1918—THE PLAYER KING
1933—MISS NOBODY FROM NOWHERE
1946—CROWN OF WILLOW
1972—LADY IN THE LIMELIGHT
1989—MY LADY DISDAIN
2044—MOUNTAIN HERITAGE
2076—AEGEAN QUEST
2093—VOYAGE OF ENCHANTMENT
2115—GREEN HARVEST
2172—BREEZE FROM THE BOSPHORUS
2179—THE QUESTING HEART
2192—THE GOLDEN GIRL

Rendezvous in Venice

by

ELIZABETH ASHTON

Harlequin Books

TORONTO • LONDON • NEW YORK • AMSTERDAM
SYDNEY • HAMBURG • PARIS

Original hardcover edition published in 1978
by Mills & Boon Limited

ISBN 0-373-02200-X

Harlequin edition published September 1978

PRINTED IN U.S.A.

CHAPTER ONE

'MY name is Camillo,' the young man said. 'You are new come to Italia, *si*?'

Shelagh Riordan glanced at her friend Gillian with a lift of her delicate eyebrows. They were 'new come', this being their first morning on the Venice Lido, the long tongue of land separating the lagoon from the Adriatic and one of the most famous playgrounds in Europe. They had been swimming and, arrayed only in their bikinis, were stretched on towels spread on the sand hoping to acquire a tan as quickly as possible. Bottles of lotion stood beside them ready to be applied to assist the process. Shelagh's white skin made her feel conspicuous among the bronzed limbs of the other holidaymakers, and proclaimed, she felt sure, her recent arrival. Gillian Dawson ignored the question in her eyes, and stared eagerly up at the young man standing over them, though his languorous dark glance was fixed upon Shelagh. They had been warned about Italian wolves, and if this was a specimen of the breed, Shelagh felt they would be wise to give him a brush-off, but he was so very good-looking that she was reluctant to do so. His olive skin was burned to a rich brown and was enhanced by his inky hair and fine dark eyes. His features were regular and when he smiled beguilingly he displayed a line of regular white teeth. A very presentable wolf, she decided, and sufficiently attractive to make intimacy with him dangerous, so that she checked her natural impulse to smile back at him in response.

Gillian had no reservations concerning him. She had

admitted en route that she hoped to pick up a boy-friend during their holiday, preferably an Italian as they were more forthcoming than British boys. This one looked as romantic as his name and he might be able to produce a friend as handsome as himself to make up a quartet.

'Yes, we are "new come",' she said with her most sexy smile. 'And feeling a little strange. Won't you sit down and tell us all the things we should see and how to set about it?'

Camillo promptly dropped down on to the sand between them. He appraised each girl in turn with a sensuous scrutiny. Gillian was brown-haired and brown-eyed with a fresh complexion, nondescript features and a full-lipped mouth, but Shelagh's hair was red-gold, and her straight nose and rounded chin were almost classical. Nature had been kind to her and bestowed upon her dark brows and lashes instead of the whitish ones that so frequently go with red hair. Her wide-set eyes were green, and she lowered her eyelashes discreetly to veil them as the young man stared rapturously at her pure profile and the tangled waves of her hair falling about her white shoulders. He lay between them on his stomach, supporting his head on his raised elbows the better to observe her.

Self-consciously Shelagh reached for her beach wrap, draped it round her and began to comb her hair. She had worn a cap, so it was not wet, only tangled, and it sprayed out from the comb like a red-gold mist. She had not yet spoken, but allowed Gillian to carry on the conversation, which she proceeded to do, providing a spate of information about themselves. They were staying at a nearby hotel and were on a package tour. She admitted frankly that they were both working girls, who shared a flat in London and liked to take their holidays together. No, Papa and Mamma were not with them. English girls preferred to take their vacations without their parents—a statement that caused Camillo to raise his straight black brows.

'We've more freedom on our own,' Gillian declared with a sly glance, 'parents can be awfully in the way at times.'

'You are fortunate yours are so accommodating,' Camillo said drily.

Shelagh could have told him that she had none to be accommodating or otherwise, being an orphan, but she saw no reason why she should mention it.

'Then if you are on your own it will be my pleasure to show you ... what do you call them ... the sights,' Camillo suggested. He spoke English with only a trace of accent.

'That would be ever so good of you,' Gillian gushed, putting on a little-girl-lost expression. 'We find everything so confusing, the money being different and not knowing the language ... all sorts of things.' She waved her hands expressively.

Shelagh smiled ironically. So far they had encountered no difficulties whatever. This being a popular tourist resort, everyone spoke some sort of English and guides were everywhere to assist them.

'I shall be happy to help you,' Camillo said gravely, but with a gleam in his eyes that proclaimed he saw through Gillian's pretences. 'Tell me, how are you called?'

Gillian hastened to inform him.

'Cheela?' he queried, looking at Shelagh, the *sh* sound being too difficult for him.

'I call her Shee.'

'Chee? No, no, I shall call you Sancia.' He looked at Shelagh ingratiatingly and she smiled faintly.

'As you please,' she returned indifferently.

Gillian too bothered his Italian tongue.

'Zut to your English names, you shall be Giulia.'

'That'll do,' Gillian conceded, 'though I'm not sold on it.'

'You have had a swim,' Camillo went on. 'What do you wish to do next?'

'Get tanned,' Shelagh told him succinctly, and reached for her bottle of lotion. She began to rub the stuff into her legs.

'It seems a pity,' Camillo complained, watching her efforts speculatively. 'That so white skin is *molta bella.*'

'Makes me feel naked,' Shelagh told him, and the glint in his expressive eyes made her wish she had chosen a less evocative word. 'It burns so quickly,' she amended, pulling her wrap more closely over her shoulders and chest. Camillo's gaze was too intimate.

Gillian also was applying tan lotion.

'I can't reach my back,' she announced with a provocative look at the young man. Camillo turned to her.

'Permette.'

Gillian handed him the bottle and turned her bare shoulders towards him. He began to lave them with the lotion and Shelagh noticed that his narrow hands were well shaped and long-fingered, but if he thought he was going to perform a similar service for herself, he was going to be disappointed. Her back must wait for its sunbath on another day. She slipped her arms into her beach wrap and tied it about her waist. It was green and white check towelling and the green matched her eyes. The torso Camillo presented to her as he performed his voluntary task was broad and bronzed, the wide shoulders tapering to a narrow waist. Stripped except for his swimming trunks, he had the figure of a Greek statue with only a faint darkening of hair on his chest, but she thought that in his clothes he might be disillusioning; young Italians taste in their gear was often too flashy.

Camillo's ministrations were accomplished with a great deal of giggling, his probing fingers making the most of his opportunity. When the operation could be protracted no longer, he turned back to Shelagh, to find she was demurely wrapped in her robe, her sunglasses perched on her nose and only her long legs revealed.

'You do not want your back rubbed?'

'No, *grazie*,' she returned, airing one of her few Italian words. 'I've exposed myself enough for one day.'

His lips curved in a bewitching smile, he had a full mouth, beautifully shaped but a little weak.

'Very circumspect, *signorina*,' he said, gently mocking.

'She's a bit of a prude,' Gillian informed him waspishly. All three knew where his interest was centred, and she was piqued.

'Scusi?' The word was unfamiliar to him.

'Standoffish,' Gillian snapped. 'Cool, frigid.'

Camillo smiled confidently. 'Not possible with that hair!'

'Don't let my colouring give you ideas,' Shelagh said sweetly.

'Me, I am most respectful.' Camillo contrived to look wounded. His eyes gleamed again. 'I like my girls, as you say, hard to get.'

'Oh, do you!' Gillian picked up her own wrap, a garish multi-coloured thing, and put it on. 'Henceforth an iceberg will have nothing on me.'

The Italian laughed and eyed her with his liquid sensual gaze.

'I wash your back,' he reminded her.

'That means nothing,' she said loftily, rising to her

feet. 'Well, what are we going to do now? Any suggestions?'

Camillo proposed going into Venice and having coffee in the Piazza San Marco.

'That entails going on a motor launch.' Shelagh looked doubtfully at the misty domes and towers across the water. 'We thought of going tomorrow when we've rested from our journey and can spend a whole day there.'

'We can cross the water in the snap of a finger and without fatigue. I have my own boat waiting for me.'

'Your own boat?' Gillian was impressed. 'Super! Let's go.'

'We'll have to put something on first,' Shelagh pointed out.

'Must we?' Gillian looked enquiringly at Camillo.

He looked a little taken aback. He had not bargained to escort two near-naked females into the city; the Italians were more conventional than the visitors when it came to dress.

'There will be many people there,' he reminded them. 'I also must clothe myself. I will come to your hotel in *un quart' ora* and conduct you to my boat. That will agree with you, *sí*?'

Gillian laughed and said it would, and told him the name of their hotel. In the room they shared, she put on slacks and a tank top, but Shelagh selected a white dress and a white hat, causing her to raise her eyebrows.

'Why this formality?'

'I think your new friend will appreciate it.'

Gillian made the expression described as a moue. 'Not my friend, unfortunately. I fancy I'm not in the running. You won't freeze him, will you, Shee? I've a hunch we're on to a good thing.'

'I promise I won't be too glacial,' Shelagh agreed.

'But I don't think we should encourage him. I've a notion these Italian boys aren't too easy to handle.'

'So long as we stick together he can't get up to any tricks,' Gillian declared. 'But don't you want to have fun?'

Shelagh wrinkled her straight nose disdainfully. 'Depends what you call fun. Signor Camillo's ideas might be different from ours.'

'Oh, we'll cope,' Gillian returned sharply, and they went out to meet their escort.

Camillo was standing on the terrace in front of their hotel looking lithe and debonair in a well-cut cream suit that looked expensive. His eyes lit up when he saw Shelagh, who made a dainty picture in her slim-fitting white dress, the crinoline hat shading her oval face, her narrow feet encased in white sandals. Below his breath he murmured:

'Bellissima!'

'Which way do we go?' Gillian demanded impatiently, for he had not looked at her, though she considered she appeared much more trendy that Shelagh.

'Please to follow me, *signorine*.' He led them down to the water front where his craft, a small gleaming motor launch, was moored in the care of a youth whom he addressed as Beppo, who had leaped ashore at their approach. With her eyes on the boat, Gillian murmured aside to Shelagh:

'Well, well, what have we picked up? Croesus?'

'I hope not Casanova,' Shelagh whispered back. She had firmly resolved that she would not allow herself to become involved with Camillo beyond the limits of courtesy, but the ardent glow in his eyes stirred her in spite of herself, and the touch of his hand as he helped her aboard sent a shiver of excitement down her spine. She told herself that he would treat every pretty girl who took his fancy with equal gallantry and tried not to feel glad that he found her more appealing than Gillian.

She sat down on the luxurious cushions that furnished the launch, and he took his place opposite to her beside Gillian, so that he could look at her, and his eyes never left her. Beppo went to the controls and the boat shot out across the Canale that separated the Lido from the city. They landed at the Molo, the steps that lead up from the water into the Piazzetta, and Shelagh felt a thrill as she beheld the pink arcaded bulk of the Palace of the Doges, recognisable from the many pictures of it she had seen. Camillo told Beppo to take the boat away and come back in an hour, and ushered them over the paving stones towards the golden façade of the Duomo San Marco, while pigeons fluttered over their heads and strutted beside their feet. The Piazzetta led into the Piazza of San Marco, which was packed with holidaymakers. Camillo adroitly steered the girls through the crowd gaping at the Palace of the Doges, and the façade of St Mark's, to a café with outdoor seating from whence they could watch the passers-by and gaze wonderingly at their surroundings.

Over glasses of iced coffee topped with cream he continued to question them about themselves, and they went into further details about their work—they were stenographers—and their microscopic flat. Respectable Italian girls, he told them, were still subject to parental control.

'But you are the new freedom girls,' he suggested with a meaning look.

'Only in that we're independent,' Shelagh said quickly. She looked him straight in the eye. 'We're not permissive.'

Gillian made a movement of protest; she appreciated her friend's motive, but she thought she might have been a little less definite. To keep Camillo guessing might persuade him to continue to offer his services and his car until he discovered he was wasting his time.

It was not the girls' first holiday abroad; they had been to Spain and there Shelagh had found it was very necessary to superintend her more impetuous friend's rash friendships. She did not want any complications with this good-looking stranger, and if she made it plain they were not available, he could drop them as suddenly as he had picked them up, if seduction were his intention.

In response to her assertion he said gallantly:

'I would not insult you by supposing you were, but what is a holiday without *l'amore*?' There was a glint in his eyes that suggested he had not entirely believed her.

'Very enjoyable,' Shelagh told him calmly. 'I'm not impressionable.'

'No, only cruel.' He turned his attention to Gillian, who was more approachable.

Shelagh watched her friend's eager response a little scornfully. If Gillian became really infatuated there was little she could do about it except prepare herself to offer what consolation she could when the inevitable heartbreak occurred, and amuse herself on her own in the meantime. Feeling excluded, she began to scan the shifting crowds of tourists. The younger ones were half naked in shorts and the mere vestige of tops, their elders, of which there was a preponderance, were well clad but perspiring.

During a temporary thinning of their ranks, a man came out of a building and strolled towards them. Instinctively the throng parted to make way for him, divining some aura of authority. Shelagh had a clear view of the straight aristocratic figure dressed in a light suit, carrying a silver-headed cane, more from affectation than because he needed it. Though past his first youth, his body was lean and agile, his face, as much as she could see of it in the shade of his panama hat, and that again marked him out where most of the men went bare-headed, was clean-shaven, hawk-nosed, with a firm mouth and chin. Shelagh's romantic fancy, ever easily touched, decided he only needed a long robe and a gold chain about his shoulders to impersonate one of the long-departed Doges.

Camillo looked round suddenly and gave an exclamation.

'Dio mio, mio papa!'

He sprang to his feet as the elder man perceived them. Shelagh saw him hesitate, then he came towards them and addressed some remark in Italian to his son.

Camillo smiled with relief as if he had been expecting censure and had received instead a compliment.

'My father wishes to be made known to you,' he said to the girls. 'Papa, this is Sancia and this Giulia.'

'Italian?'

'No, Papa, that is my version of their so difficult names. Ladies, may I present Signore Cesare Barsini, my father.'

Signore Barsini took off his hat with a flourish and bowed. His hair was crisp and black with a tendency to curl. His thick eyebrows covered eyes that to her surprise Shelagh saw were grey. He had the head of a Roman emperor set arrogantly upon his broad shoulders. Camillo's air was deferential; he was obviously proud of his father. Cesare Barsini gave Gillian a cursory glance, but his eyes lingered upon Shelagh. When she met his keen penetrating gaze she was aware of acute discomfort, for there was a question in it, as if he were wondering how and why she had allowed herself to be picked up by his son. She also had an impression that it was by no means the first time that he had encountered Camillo in the company of strange women, and that he did not regard his son's favours as a compliment to any nice girl; but when he spoke his words were flowery.

'Camillo has shown his usual good taste,' he said suavely, and his voice was deep and pleasant with no trace of accent. 'You are both enchanting.'

Gillian simpered, but Shelagh flushed and turned away her head. Unreasonably she wanted to tell him that it was not her usual practice to associate with strange men, although her habits could be of no possible interest to him.

Camillo indicated a vacant chair. 'Will you join us, Papa?'

Cesare shook his head. 'You do not wish for the repression of my presence,' he told them with a wry smile. 'And I must be on my way. *Ciao.*'

He bowed again, replacing his hat. Again he gave Shelagh a searching look, then he walked away with a swift supple stride.

'What was that for?' Gillian asked. 'An inspection parade?'

Camillo grinned impishly. 'Papa likes to put tickets on my lady friends,' he informed them. 'It would seem he approves of Sancia.' He glanced at Shelagh. 'He also admires red hair.'

'He couldn't see much of it under my hat,' Shelagh remarked, still under the influence of Cesare Barsini's disquieting gaze. 'And I think you've got it wrong. From his expression he disapproved of me entirely.'

'Impossible!' Camillo exclaimed. 'He was all of admiration. I am glad he is gone or I might be jealous.'

'Oh, don't be silly!' Shelagh was annoyed by such an

uncalled-for observation. Then, realising she had been rude, she asked:

'Do your parents live in Venice?'

'My mother is dead,' Camillo said shortly.

'Oh, I'm sorry.'

'No need for grief, I never knew her. She died when I was born, and Papa married again.'

'So you have a stepmother?'

'Not now. She too is dead. Papa has the bad fortune in matrimony. I have a half-sister, that is all—but enough of me.' He looked intently at Shelagh. 'You have a lover in England, *si*? That is why you are so cold?'

'No, I've no boy-friends,' she replied, then wished that she had claimed one, as it might have saved future complications.

'So you are ... what does the poet say ... footloose and fancy free?' he demanded triumphantly.

She smiled. 'You could say that, and I've every intention of remaining so.'

'Chi lo sa!' he said meaningfully.

Feeling neglected, Gillian moved restlessly.

'When you two've finished gazing into each other's eyes, what do we do next?' she demanded. 'I want to go in a gondola, isn't that the thing to do in Venice?'

They went in a gondola. Camillo insisted upon being their guide, also upon giving them lunch. Shelagh was a little disappointed with Venice. Although the old palaces were still beautiful, the whole place looked a little shabby and neglected. There were far too many visitors and motor craft exuding fumes of petrol and diesel oil.

'It must have been lovely in the old days before it was spoilt,' she said to Camillo.

'When the Doges used to wed the sea with rings?' he suggested. 'Venezia la Serenissima she used to be called, but the days of her glory are over, she is sinking back into the sea. *Sic transit gloria mundi* and all that. Myself, I prefer what is new and modern. The Barsinis own an island in the archipelago, there are many islets towards the sea, and Papa shuts himself up there with his books and his music. I do not often go there, it is too sad.'

'He grieves for his wife, perhaps?'

Camillo shrugged his shoulders. 'That is an old story. No, it is the way he chooses to live, for the fire of youth is dead in him; in me it is aflame.'

His glance was amorous.

'Don't be too sure about that,' Gillian said unexpectedly. 'Your father isn't old yet. He looked to me to be capable of ... anything.' She giggled.

'It is as I say,' Camillo insisted. 'There are many women who would gladly lighten his loneliness and be a mother to his *figlia*, for my sister Margarita is still a child, but he is impervious to feminine wiles.'

Since both his marriages had ended tragically, he might well be reluctant to try again, Shelagh thought, but he appeared to be still strong and vigorous. Doubtless some woman shared his seclusion on his island in the Adriatic, unknown even to his son, since he rarely went there. Then she gave herself a mental shake. In all probability she would never meet Cesare Barsini again, and his way of life was of no interest to her, except that his proud Roman head and arrogant carriage had made a lasting impression. Of more consequence there was the son with whom to deal, who seemed determined to continue their acquaintanceship. He knew there would be dancing at their hotel in the evening after dinner and announced his intention of joining them.

'Me, I waltz most excellently,' he boasted, his black eyes dancing.

'Don't you know anything more modern?' Gillian enquired.

'*Ecco*, I know them all, but I like best the waltz. It is so romantic to hold one's partner close in one's arms to the sound of soft music.' His eyes were eloquent.

'Quite so,' Gillian agreed, 'but you can't hold us both in your arms.'

'That shall be arranged,' he declared. 'I will bring another dancer most excellent, then all will be satisfied.'

'Now you've done it,' Shelagh complained, when he had left them at their hotel at siesta time. 'We'll have two Italian wolves to contend with and it'll be much more difficult if we get paired off.'

'Difficult my foot,' Gillian snapped. 'It's obvious Casanova's got his eye on you, and I don't fancy playing gooseberry all evening. If he produces someone as good-looking as himself I shan't shout for help. When he looks at me so soulfully my heart actually melts.'

'So long as you remember that he doesn't mean anything except perhaps bed,' Shelagh warned her.

'But I enjoy playing with fire,' Gillian declared.

'Then you've only yourself to blame if you get burnt.'

'Stop it!' Gillian cried. 'You're talking like a Victorian maiden aunt. We're on holiday, Shee, and we're here to have fun, and fun I mean to have.'

The 'dancer most excellent' was nearly as good-looking as Camillo, a slim brown youth called Alonso, with melting brown eyes. With his advent, Camillo's manner towards Shelagh became proprietorial. He made it quite plain that Alonso's role was to console Gillian, and after one or two wistful glances towards Shelagh's red-gold hair, Alonso accepted his fate. Gillian was looking very pretty, wearing a long printed dress in colours of brown, white and pink that toned with her complexion and her hair, but Shelagh, in a gold-coloured sheath with her shining hair loose about her face, was a flame to fire a man's desire, as Camillo told her, his black eyes alight with passion.

She found it was impossible to maintain her attitude of aloof indifference as the evening progressed. The music and his proximity excited her and his touch thrilled her. He was the handsomest man in the room, elegant in dark trousers and white jacket with an air of distinction that most of the other men lacked. Having seen his father, she suspected that he must be an aristocrat, a realisation that disturbed her, for an Italian of noble descent could have no honest intentions towards a London typist. But as time passed, she forgot her misgivings, surrendering to the sensuous Italian night, the close contact of his arms and the ardour in his eloquent eyes. That the other girls were envying her her partner added to her enjoyment.

She made him dance once with Gillian, insisting that it was only polite to do so, and he left her but with reluctance. Alonso, delighted by the exchange, extolled his friend's good luck.

'If only I had met you first,' he sighed.

Alonso rather repelled her. He had all Camillo's amorousness without his charm. Though a lot of younger people were performing their own gymnastics, the Italian men preferred to waltz or foxtrot if the music permitted it. As Camillo had said, Alonso also declared: 'When I dance I like to hold my girl in my arms.

'Most so when she looka like you,' he added. His English was not as good as his friend's. Shelagh was relieved when Camillo came back to claim her. If she had to be pressed to a manly bosom she would rather it were his. The long windows of the room were wide open to the warm night, spangled with stars. Couples disappeared from time to time to indulge in necking sessions, but in spite of Camillo's persuasions, Shelagh refused to go outside.

'I wish to melt your ice,' he told her bluntly.

'I daresay, but I'm not ready to melt,' she returned. 'After all, Camillo, I only met you this morning—you're going too fast.'

'Am I?' He gave her a long considering look. They were sitting at the side of the room under a potted palm. 'Life is so short, little one,' he went on plaintively. 'I want to snatch at the good things too quick.' He smiled charmingly. 'But we will wait until you know me better, then perhaps you trust me, *sí*? Now you think I am, what you call, a big bad wolf, *no*?'

'Well ...' She hesitated, for that was what she had thought.

'Then I must be a very good boy.' He sighed. 'But you will come with me tomorrow, *sí*? We go out in my car, a long way without your friend.'

'I can't leave Gill,' Shelagh protested. 'We're here together, it wouldn't be fair.'

'Alonso will take care of her,' he told her arrogantly.

'Now look here.' Shelagh roused herself from the sensuous spell he was weaving around her. 'You can't order everyone about to suit your convenience. Gill mayn't want to be packed off with your friend, or he with her. If we go anywhere we go together.'

He gave her a mischievous look. 'It will arrange itself.'

It did, or rather Camillo did. In the days that followed he organised their amusements and expeditions and invariably Shelagh found herself escorted by him. There was always someone for Gillian, if not Alonso some other youth, and several times he organised parties with several young couples for bathing or dancing, but Shelagh always found herself beside him in his car or in his arms at a dance.

'Are you having an affair?' Gillian asked her bluntly one night at the end of their first week.

'You know I'm not. I always refuse to go out with him alone.'

'He's getting restive,' Gillian warned her. 'Soon you'll have to face a showdown. He looks at you as if he could eat you, and he must have spent quite a lot of money on our entertainment. He'll expect to be paid for that.'

Shelagh had been troubled herself about the amount of money that Camillo flung around so lavishly, but she said disdainfully:

'Must you doubt his motives? He says he's lonely, some girl has let him down. He's on holiday too and he enjoys our company.'

For so Camillo had told her, though she only half believed him, for what girl in her right mind would turn down a rich and handsome young man unless he had demanded more than she was prepared to give. She went in daily dread of the same alternative being put to herself, for she would be hard put to it to resist his Italian charm. She had never been in love before, but she seemed to be well on the way to it now. Camillo's melting glances, his soft caressing voice stirred her blood, and when he touched her she was conscious of a rising excitement, a tingling of her nerves, but she knew there was no future for them; it was merely a holiday flirtation that must not be allowed to get out of hand.

The crisis came during an expedition to Murano to look at the glass factory. Finding the heat overpowering, Shelagh had murmured an excuse to go outside and leave the rest of the party inside. Almost immediately Camillo came to join her.

'It would be cooler in the mountains,' he observed. 'And the lakes are beautiful. Will you not come with me for a few days to enjoy their scenery? Just you and I, *carissima,* without these tiresome friends.'

'Sounds beautiful, Camillo, but it isn't possible,' Shelagh told him quietly.

'All things are possible when one loves.'

'You're being absurd. You can't fall in love in a few days,' she declared, while her heart beat fast and she was almost painfully aware of him beside her, his dark head and beautiful face inclined towards her, and the burning intensity of his gaze.

'But I have,' he said softly. 'And you ... you like me, *sí*?'

She roused herself with an effort.

'Camillo, I do like you, but I can't ... I mean, I'm a good girl. If that's what you want from me I'm afraid you're wasting your time and your money.'

'But you would not wish to never see me again?' His eloquent eyes were beseeching.

'That's emotional blackmail,' she told him with a wan smile. Summoning all her resolution, she went on firmly, 'I would be sorry not to see you again, but I can only give you friendship. If that's not enough, then it must be goodbye.'

She could not control a quiver in her voice as she realised how devastatingly she would miss him.

'You are afraid, is it not so?' he asked gently. 'You have no experience of love? Let me teach you.'

He drew her into his arms, but with all her strength she pushed him away from her, though her senses were clamouring for his embrace.

'No, Camillo, no, please!' she cried in a panic.

He drew back and said scornfully, 'For whom do you save yourself? Some man in England?'

'For my husband, when I have one,' she said simply.

'But you say you are not betrothed?'

'No, but I might be, some day. Oh, Camillo, can't you see, you're making me so cheap!'

He looked at her ruefully. 'It is most strange. I thought the English ... the tourists ... expect love as part of the package holiday.'

She was not surprised he thought that, after the way Gillian encouraged men. She said steadily:

'Perhaps some do, but I'm not one of them.'

He came to her and took her face between his hands, gazing into her eyes as if he would read her very soul. She returned his regard without faltering, her eyes very green in her pale face.

'*Si!*' he exclaimed vehemently. 'You *are* different—you are pure, innocent, in spite of all this freedom.'

'That's about it,' she concurred, blushing a little at the way he put it.

He dropped his hands and turned away frowning.

'It is my bad luck.'

As she glanced at his carved profile, Shelagh's heart sank. After today she would see no more of her cavalier. Almost she contemplated surrender; a few days alone in the Italian Alps with him would be heaven, but the aftermath would be unbearable, he would leave her desolate, for she knew instinctively that she could not give her heart lightly.

Presently Camillo looked at her and his eyes were misted with emotion.

'But I love you ... what am I to do?'

She voiced the painful alternative.

'It would be best if you didn't see me again.'

'Ah, little hard heart!' He snatched her hand and kissed it fervently, his lips travelling up her wrist and bare arm. '*Amore mia,*' he murmured thickly. '*Amore mia!*'

The rest of the party came straggling towards them, and Camillo dropped her arm.

'I will think of something,' he assured her, and went to greet his friends.

He did not suggest any outing for the following day, nor did he appear in the evening. Gillian and Shelagh danced with the hotel guests, but Shelagh's eyes were forever travelling towards the entrance, seeking for a black head and lean, lithe figure. One of her partners, a British boy also on tour, became too fresh and she slapped his face. The action relieved her pent feelings, and she went outside to sit by herself in a dark corner from which she could hear the murmur of the sea, and see the lights of Venice on the further shore. Was she really in love with Camillo or merely infatuated by his good looks? She did not know, it did not seem possible on such a short acquaintanceship, but she did know she missed him sorely.

Next morning there was still no sign of Camillo or any of his friends, and Shelagh went with Gillian to the lido to bathe.

'Did something happen at Murano?' Gillian asked, eyeing her shrewdly. Even Shelagh's newly acquired tan could not conceal her pallor and there were dark marks under her eyes. She had slept little while she strove to sort out her mixed emotions.

'Only the inevitable,' she said wearily. 'I wouldn't play ball.'

'Don't you think you're being stupidly old-fashioned?' Gillian asked. 'He would be a wonderful lover, I'm sure, and nowadays nobody would blame you. You miss such a lot by being priggish.'

'I couldn't,' Shelagh told her. 'To be picked up and dropped ... a holiday affair ... I'm sure love should be more than that.'

'You'll lose him,' Gillian warned.

'I have,' Shelagh said grimly. 'Let's swim.'

But afterwards as she lay on the beach, he turned up. Her body was tanning nicely, a golden girl with the glow of autumn in her outspread hair. Camillo stood beside her, a towel draped over his naked shoulders, his eyes kindling as they travelled over her long slender limbs. Shelagh stared up at him unbelievingly; she had not expected to see him again. Had he come back to renew his importunities, and could she resist him if he did?

'Last night I think and think and walk and walk,' he told her. He flung out his hand dramatically, and his expression became triumphant. 'The answer come to me. There is only one thing we can do, for I cannot bear to lose you.' He dropped to his haunches beside her. '*Carissima,* we must be married.'

CHAPTER TWO

SHELAGH RIORDAN, presumed to be an orphan, had been raised at a convent school. Before her birth, the establishment had taken on as kitchenmaid an Irish immigrant, by name Eileen O'Riordan. As usual they were short of staff, so the Sisters did not ask too many questions, but Eileen in spite of lack of references proved to be honest and industrious. Bit by bit her history came out. She had come to London at sixteen hoping to better herself, but being very young and innocent fell into bad company. With difficulty she had extricated herself and fled into the country for refuge. She had been destitute when she applied to the convent for work and the Mother Superior said they could not turn her away. She was very devout, and the Mother Superior, detecting in her refinement and intelligence, tried to win her confidence, but Eileen refused to divulge anything about her family.

'They are dead to me and I can never go back,' she declared. 'They must never know the life I led in London.'

'You were more sinned against than sinning,' Mother Cecilia insisted. 'And if you truly repent they will forgive you.'

But Eileen was adamant. She was an Irish beauty, raven-haired and blue-eyed, but she had no use for men.

'They're horrible,' she said, and shuddered.

She worked at the convent lodging in the hostel attached to it. It was a teaching order and ran its own boarding school of carefully vetted pupils. The Sisters were at first careful that the new kitchenmaid should have no contact with their élite clientele, but her behaviour was so exemplary that she was promoted to other duties.

Then after two years, as suddenly as she had come, she went.

'I'm going to be married,' she told the nun who did the housekeeping.

Mother Cecilia asked to see her. 'Who is the young man?' she asked kindly.

'No one you know.' Eileen's manner was almost defiant.

With deep misgiving they had no option but to let her go.

The Mother Superior told her, 'If ever you need help come to us again.'

'Thank you, but my husband will take care of me from now on,' Eileen said confidently.

About eighteen months later the nuns discovered outside the main door a three-month-old baby in a basket, with a label about her neck. On it was written:

'Her name is Shelagh. For the love of God give her the help you offered to me.'

Eileen's child? Presumably. The nuns went into consultation. They were a school, not an orphanage.

Sister Joanna of the Cross was emphatic. 'We can't keep her. Think what the parents will say when our pupils tell them we have adopted the daughter of a slut whose second name we don't know!'

Mother Cecilia told her, 'We have to teach them tolerance and charity. This child has been given to us as a sacred trust. She stays.'

Since it was not known if she had been baptised, the child was christened Shelagh Riordan and was reared by the nuns and educated at the convent school. Nothing further was heard of Eileen, nor was Shelagh told that she might still be alive. She was informed that she had been found outside the convent, 'a gift from God', and that was all. As she grew older she realised that that meant she had been abandoned, but the knowledge did not embitter her, for she adored Mother Cecilia, who she considered to be an earthly saint, and the Mother Superior herself called herself her 'spiritual mother'. In her early teens, Shelagh imagined she had a vocation, but Mother Cecilia discouraged her.

'You are too young to know your own mind. Wait, my daughter, and pray for guidance.'

At sixteen she changed her mind; the world was too alluring and exciting to renounce. She learned typing and shorthand, and had her first job in a small town near the convent, moving eventually to a more lucrative post in London. There she left the hostel where she lodged after a few months to share a small flatlet with Gillian Dawson, who worked in the same office and had become a special friend. But the convent had marked her; she possessed a serenity and detachment that made her appear different from her restless pleasure-seeking colleagues. Gillian often teased her about her convent inhibitions which prevented her, she declared, from fully enjoying life, by which she meant boy-friends, but Shelagh, who was fastidious, did not care for the brash young men who tried to date her.

'They're only after one thing,' she said contemptuously, 'and that I'll never give without love.'

'But how can you fall in love if you live like a nun?'

'I was brought up like one, and there are worse ways of living,' Shelagh returned imperturbably.

And now she was in love with a fascinating Italian boy who wanted to marry her. It seemed to be the realisation of all her romantic dreams, for naturally she had not reached twenty without having had them. And as in the best romances, there were snags. She had no kin, no background, and no dowry, which she understood was usual with continental brides. Camillo's father was the handsome aristocrat to whom he had introduced her in the Piazza at Venice, who surely would never countenance such a match for his only son, for whom he must desire a great alliance.

She tried to express her doubts and fears to Camillo, but he brushed them aside.

'I am in love with *you*, not your background or your family. I am not tied to my papa's coat tails, and since there is no other way to have you, he will understand we must be married.'

Not a very good reason for forming a permanent connection, but Shelagh was too besotted to consider that. She found it sweet to be so passionately desired, and love made her glow with a beauty that inflamed him and made even Gillan remark upon it.

'I've never seen your eyes look so green or your hair so red,' she said peevishly.

'Carrots?' Shelagh suggested.

'No, Shee, more like molten gold and copper. Fact is, I'm jealous.'

'Gill, you haven't fallen for him too?'

'I could have done. Oh well, there's always Alonso, and I'll be able to spend my holidays with you when you're married.'

'You'll be welcome.' But she could not quite believe in that marriage. Everything had happened so quickly she could not visualise herself as Camillo's wife.

Her response to Camillo's lovemaking had been overwhelming, and she was shocked and dismayed by the strength of her own emotions, but there was rapture also. A whole new world opened before her, but she continued to insist that fulfilment must wait until they were married. To anticipate it, she declared, would be a pity, making the great day an anti-climax. Camillo agreed, but insisted she must not make him wait too long.

Gillian applauded her caution, as she called it. She considered her friend had been phenomenally lucky to hook such a rich husband, and admitted that playing hard to get sometimes paid dividends. Shelagh disliked Gillian's attitude; she had had no mercenary motives in her treatment of Camillo, but an instinctive recoil from casual embraces. She loved him and wanted to give herself, but she wanted it to be permanent. If love did not rate marriage it could not be true love. To her it was as simple as that.

Camillo told her his father wished to see her and had asked him to bring her to visit him at his island retreat. Though she realised that as his son's fiancée she must pay her respects to Cesare, Shelagh viewed the proposed expedition with trepidation. She was certain the elder Barsini would make difficulties, even try to part them, and he would question her about her background and be dismayed by her revelations.

'You won't let him come between us?' she asked Camillo anxiously.

'*Dio mio*, most certainly not!' he reassured her. 'But you are over-fearful, *cara*, he is not an ogre and he believes marriage will be good for me, a stabilising influence.' He laughed scornfully. 'When he discovers how sweet and good you are he will be most pleased.'

Shelagh doubted that virtue and an amicable temperament could counterbalance a lack of dowry and connections in Cesare's eyes, but meet him she must and rely upon Camillo to support her.

So one afternoon they set forth in the motorboat, which incidentally Camillo told her had been his father's present to him on his twenty-first birthday, information that made Shelagh open her eyes very wide. The Barsinis must indeed be affluent to give such valuable presents. She wore navy slacks as being suitable for a boat trip, with a white and navy striped tee-shirt, her golden hair confined by a silk handkerchief. Camillo was similarly attired, except that his colours were red and black. He looked debonair and dangerous, his thick hair ruffled by the breeze and his eyes glittering with excitement aroused by the speed of their passage, as the boat clove the water like an arrow, with a reckless disregard of other craft.

The Isola di Santa Lucia was one of the many islets situated where the Lagoon merged with the Adriatic, and was surrounded by a screen of trees and shrubs. After disembarking at the landing stage, Camillo led Shelagh along a winding path through a mass of bushes, some in flower, which she could not identify. It ended in a vast expanse of lawn, decorated with flower beds full of exotic blooms, and white statues, copies of famous pieces of sculpture of classical design, in the centre of which a fountain played, its spray gleaming in the sunlight. Across on its further side was the house, a long white building fronted by a colonnade of pillars supporting a balcony, and giving shade to a wide terrace approached by steps. Shelagh gazed at it awestruck.

'Cam, it's a palace!'

He shrugged his shoulders. 'Hardly that, and it's modern. Papa likes his comfort. The plumbing is excellent—and expensive to maintain.'

'I don't doubt it.'

She noticed as they walked across the lawn that there was a swimming pool to one side of the house, and tennis courts on the other. As a holiday resort it was perfect.

It was about four o'clock in the afternoon, the siesta time over, and as they approached the colonnade Shelagh saw there were loungers and canvas chairs set out on the terrace beneath it, and from one of them Cesare stood up to receive them. He wore cream-coloured trousers and jacket of perfect cut, and a blue tie over his white silk shirt. His black hair, slightly tinged with grey at the temples, was cut short, showing the shape of his patrician head. He looked every inch a great gentleman.

'*Benvenuto,*' he said in his deep resonant voice, while his keen grey eyes took in every detail of her appearance. He held out his hand as she timidly confronted him, and she laid hers within it, glancing curiously at the strong brown fingers clasping hers. Cesare must be forty at least, but he showed no sign of age and bore himself with a fine air of distinction.

He made her sit in a chair beside him and as if on cue, a manservant appeared carrying a tray of drinks.

'You would like some refreshment, Signorina Riordan?' he enquired courteously, and she was surprised that he remembered her surname.

'*Si, per piacere,*' she said, tremulously aware of his continued scrutiny, hoping he admired red hair.

'You speak Italian?'

She smiled. 'That's about the extent of my vocabulary.'

'Then of course you will have to learn to speak it fluently.'

'I'll do my best.'

From the tray offered to her she took lemon and ice.

'Would you not prefer something stronger to fortify yourself?' Camillo suggested mischievously, taking a brandy and soda.

'No, thank you, and I'm sure I shan't need Dutch

courage.' She looked appealingly at Cesare, who had resumed his seat beside her, but his face remained inscrutable. He had dropped his eyes and she noticed how long and thick were the lashes surrounding them.

They made rather stilted small talk. Camillo lounged against a pillar, glass in hand, watching her critically. She wondered how she was making out with his papa, but the grey eyes in the carved olive face betrayed nothing except polite interest in her trite remarks. Camillo was regarding her with an insolent possessiveness that vaguely disturbed her. She did not belong to him yet and she expected opposition from his parent. He had not told her how far he was dependent upon him, and if Cesare sent her packing he might lose a lot. Would he consider her worth it?

As she finished her drink, Cesare said:

'Camillo, please to remove yourself. I wish to speak to this young lady alone.'

Camillo's dark brows drew together and his eyes smouldered suspiciously. 'Why so, Papa? Do you intend to put her against me?'

'I do not imagine I could do that,' Cesare said drily. 'But I wish to get to know her, as she is to become my daughter-in-law. She will not give me her confidence while you stand there glaring at me as if my intentions were dishonourable—besides, I require her undivided attention.'

Shelagh wilted inwardly. This sounded ominous; there was something very intimidating about this suave, imperious gentleman. She had no wish whatever to be left alone with him. He went on:

'I am your father, boy, and I have your welfare very much at heart, also hers.'

He threw Shelagh an enigmatical glance, and meeting it, she lifted her head proudly, her courage returning in a sudden flood. She would not allow him to browbeat her; she was fit to be any man's wife, healthy, honest and virtuous. If he did not like her circumstances, that would be just too bad—for him. It flashed into her mind that he might be about to insult her by attempting to buy her off; the thought gave an angry sparkle to her green eyes and her mouth set obstinately. A glint of admiration came into the elder man's eyes before he looked away.

Camillo apparently had similar doubts to her own, for he said truculently:

'*Benissimo,* Papa *mio,* but nothing you say will alter anything. I am going to marry her.'

With which assertion he flung out of the colonnade and disappeared round the corner of the house while his father watched him frowning.

'Impetuous and unstable,' he murmured more to himself than to the girl beside him, but Shelagh was not listening; she was trying to find the right words to soften him towards herself. She said quietly:

'You've a right to ask me anything I can tell you and I know very well I'm not the sort of daughter-in-law you desire. I'm only a very ordinary English girl and I've no money or prospects.'

'You do not look in the least ordinary,' he returned with his eyes on her hair. 'As for money and prospects, is that why you want my son? He has both.'

'Certainly not!' she cried indignantly. 'They're not important.' Cesare smiled sardonically. 'I ... I love Camillo.'

'You are sure of it?'

'Quite sure,' she returned confidently.

'You've known him ... how long?'

'Can one measure love by time? It came suddenly—devastatingly.'

'It might be only infatuation.'

'Isn't that much the same thing?'

'No, because you don't know him and you are not seeing him as he really is, but only your image of him.' He looked away across the brilliant garden. 'I myself married at eighteen against my parents' wishes. She was very beautiful, but as I subsequently discovered, completely empty-headed. After six months I was bored to death with her.'

'After only six months?' Shelagh was shocked.

'You find that incredible? But a boy's passion can be soon appeased. Of course, had she lived, our children would have bound us together, but she was a silly woman.'

'You believe Camillo will tire of me in six months?' Shelagh asked in a choked voice. He had been describing Camillo's mother.

He smiled. 'You are not a silly woman, but you may tire of him.'

Recalling her handsome romantic lover, she cried emphatically:

'That's impossible!'

'You are so sure after such a brief acquaintanceship?'

'Well, of course we aren't proposing to get married tomorrow,' she laughed shakily. 'We'll have to get to know each other a bit better first.'

But Camillo was insistent that he could not wait—long.

Shelagh wondered at the direction in which the conversation had moved. She had expected questions about her parentage, her way of life, instead of which he had confided in her the failure of his own first marriage. Then she thought she understood. Cesare was too clever to directly oppose them, he was seeking to undermine her confidence by more subtle means; he would be a dangerous and skilful adversary.

'You could say Camillo has swept me off my feet,' she

went on, 'but I've never ever remotely felt about anyone else as I do about him. I'm sure it must be the real thing.'

Even to herself the words sounded trite and naïve, but somehow she must convince this worldly man of the wonderful thing that had happened to her.

'You are . . . how old?'

'Just twenty.'

'Mere infants, both of you, with your heads full of romantic nonsense.' The grey eyes mocked her.

'Youth is the time for loving, as the song says,' she pointed out. She smiled sweetly. 'We'll grow up together, and aren't all marriages a bit of a gamble? Isn't it a good basis to start with a great passion?' She looked at Cesare appealingly, her eyes very green.

'You plead well, little witch,' he said softly, 'but you are not Camillo's first great passion.'

'What happened to the others?' she asked, trying to speak lightly, though the information was unwelcome.

'They faded.'

Remembering Gillian's approval of her abstinence, she asked bluntly:

'After consummation?'

'You are crude, *signorina.*'

'But that's the truth, isn't it? *Signore,* I respect myself too much to have an affair with Camillo.'

'Perhaps it would be better for you if you did, but then you would gain nothing except heartbreak, whereas if he marries you, you will have much to compensate you if he is unfaithful.'

Shelagh sprang to her feet her face flaming, her eyes sparkling.

'*Signore,* I'm not mercenary. I told you before I'm not interested in wealth. I'd marry Camillo if he hadn't a penny. Actually I don't know what he has got, and I imagine you can cut him off if you don't approve. But I hope you won't, because ... because ...' she faltered and stopped, the colour ebbing from her face leaving her very pale. She turned her head and stared unseeingly out over the brilliance of the garden. Cesare was gazing appreciatively at her pure profile outlined against the darker background. The girl was ridiculously immature, but she could be moulded, by the right hand, and she had a wistful sensitive beauty that only a connoisseur could fully appreciate. Not Camillo's usual type at all, he liked his women buxom, but she had fire and spirit, so perhaps that was what had attracted him. She might, she just might be able to hold him. He said deliberately:

'You are afraid that he would think disinheritance too high a price to pay for you?'

She made a little helpless gesture with one hand.

'I don't know.' She swung round to face him, her mobile face accusing. 'Are you our enemy, *signore*?'

'Not at all. Sit down, Signorina Riordan. With that coloured hair you are naturally fiery, but I have given you no cause to fight me ... yet.' His stern face broke into a sudden sweet smile. '*Dio mio,* I could envy that young reprobate!'

Something in his appraising stare caused her heart to flutter. He had reached his forties, but he was still a handsome, virile man, who had worn well. A half-formed thought crossed her mind; if she could charm him, she might be able to lessen his antagonism, for though he had denied it she was certain he did not approve of the marriage. But she could not bring herself to stoop to coquetry, not with Camillo's father. Abruptly she told him:

'My mother was a housemaid ... *una cameriera,* I believe you call it.'

He raised his dark level brows. 'And your father?'

She shrugged her shoulders. 'No one knows.'

Officially she had been told her parents were unknown, but one day when she had annoyed her, Sister Joanna had informed her of her mother's status and been given a stern penance for doing so.

Cesare studied her for some moments in silence, noting her long clean limbs and well set head. Leaning forward, he picked up her hand and encircled her fine wrist with his other hand.

'You have not the bones or the complexion of a peasant.'

She coloured faintly under her thin skin, very conscious of the touch of his slender but muscular fingers.

'It's no good inventing a noble father for me—he was probably a rogue.'

'*Basta,* I know good blood when I see it.' He dropped her wrist. 'Camillo tells me you are convent-bred. You could not have had a better training for matrimony, and a good wife may sober my son. I will not disguise from you that he has been a little wild. The responsibility of a wife and family may induce him to settle down, but you are taking a risk.'

She said with innocent simplicity: 'Since we love each other I'm willing to take a chance on him.'

'The sublime confidence of youth!' Cesare exclaimed, and sighed.

'Oh, you're a cynic,' she told him angrily, 'just because...'

The quick patter of small feet interrupted her and a little girl of about eight years old came running out from the interior of the house and hurled herself upon Cesare, uttering a spate of Italian.

'Rita, Rita, where are your manners?' her father expostulated. 'We have a guest.'

The child seated upon his knees turned round and

stared at Shelagh. Then she buried her face in his shoulder as if overcome by shyness. She was small for her age, thin and brown with a bush of dark hair, but her eyes were a clear grey like Cesare's.

'My daughter, Margarita,' he introduced her. 'Rita, this is the lady who is to marry Camillo.'

The child lifted her head to stare again at Shelagh, then she made some comment in her own language that caused her father to grimace.

'Speak English,' he commanded. 'Say how are you.'

'Comé 'sta?' Rita returned obediently, then very carefully: ''Ow do you do?'

'Very well, thank you,' Shelagh responded solemnly. 'And you?'

Rita ducked her head again. 'Fine,' she murmured.

'Her English is very good,' Shelagh observed politely.

'Fine is I believe American,' Cesare complained. 'She has an English governess ... what is it, *bimba*?'

Rita wanted to know if she could go swimming.

Cesare pushed her off his knees. 'In the pool, not the lagoon! Do you swim, *signorina* ... by the way, I am told your name is Sancia. Since you are to become one of the family, I shall call you by it.'

So obliquely he was letting her know that he had accepted her, but she pointed out that her name was Shelagh, and she preferred it to Camillo's Sancia. She did not mention that as it was his name for her she did not want anyone else to use it.

'Sancia goes better with Barsini,' Cesare observed, and she felt a sudden qualm. She would be expected to renounce her country and she had not yet considered the full implication of that, and he was reminding her. This man was full of Latin cunning and his stabs would never be direct, would he while apparently acquiescent work against her in the dark? He met her troubled gaze with bland serenity, and she could not gauge if it were sincere.

Rita reiterated her intention of going for a swim, adding:

'Will you accompany me, *signorina*?' The quaint formality of her request indicated that the English governess did not neglect her duties.

'I haven't brought a swimsuit,' Shelagh demurred.

'One shall be found for you,' Cesare told her. 'Rita, take the Signorina indoors to the guest room and ask Giovanna for *una costume da bagno*.'

The costume Giovanna, who turned out to be the housekeeper, produced was a green regulation type garment; it was hardly probable there would be a bikini in that household. The room Rita took Shelagh into was plainly but beautifully furnished on the ground floor. She had barely had time to change when the child came prancing in again wearing a microscopic version of her own costume.

'You like to swim?' she demanded. 'With me?'

'Very much.'

'We take towels.' She swept a couple of beautiful white towels off a rail by the fitted basin and ran towards the french window that gave access to the terrace.

Camillo, having been informed of their intention, came to join them in the pool wearing trunks. He scowled at his half-sister, addressing her sharply in Italian. Rita appealed to Shelagh.

'You said you like to swim with me.'

'I told her to go inside,' Camillo said sulkily. 'We don't want her bothering us.'

'But she's no bother,' Shelagh said quickly as Rita's lip quivered. 'Her father said she should show me round, and I like having her.'

'That is more than I do,' Camillo muttered below

his breath. Then he smiled sunnily. 'It is as you wish, *carissima.*'

Shelagh wondered with dismay if he did not like children, but now was not the time to go into that. Rita said in an undertone:

'I hate *mio fratello.*'

'Race you to the other side!' Shelagh cried, diving into the pool, which was a big one, puzzling as she did so what could lie behind this aversion between brother and sister. Italians were so fond of children, she had always understood, or was that a fallacy?

Rita swam like a seal and Shelagh had some difficulty in keeping up with her. They reached the further side breathless and laughing to find Cesare had strolled out to watch them.

'I won!' Rita cried as he reached down to take her hands and pull her up over the edge of the pool. Shelagh, standing in the water, for it was shallow at that end, with her wet hair clinging to her neck and shoulders, laughed up at them.

'I think it was neck-and-neck.'

Cesare's eyes were upon her slight figure revealed by her wet costume with a disconcerting glint in their grey depths.

'It seems we have imported a mermaid.'

Camillo came swooping towards them underwater. He seized Shelagh's knees and she fell over with a splash. Crying: 'Oh, you wretch!' she streaked after him across the pool, while Cesare absently stroked Rita's damp head.

'Love's young dream,' he murmured in his own tongue. 'Always so refreshing and so short-lived.'

'I hope Camillo does not live long,' Rita said with Latin vindictiveness. 'He is horrid!'

'You must not be so melodramatic,' Cesare said severely. 'Our guest likes Camillo, *bimba,* and who knows? Perhaps she can redeem him. Love has been known to perform miracles.'

This was too profound for Rita.

'Watch me dive, Papa,' she commanded, and plunged into the pool.

CHAPTER THREE

CONTRARY to Shelagh's expectations, Cesare did not actively oppose his son's marriage to an insignificant English girl, but he made conditions. It was not to take place until the following spring and in the meantime, Shelagh should return to England while Camillo concentrated upon a job to provide for her.

The Barsinis had wide business interests, their principal trade being export with their headquarters at Genoa, or Genova as the Italians call it. It was Cesare's intention that Camillo should represent him at the Genoese offices, where he also ran a boatbuilding concern, where his son's motor launch had been made. There was a handsome house outside the city which he would give the young couple as a wedding present. Since leaving collage, Camillo had enjoyed a playboy existence, his father allowing him a recreation period before settling down to work, but now that he was contemplating becoming a family man, Cesare insisted he must assume both financial and personal responsibilities.

Cesare's arrangements seemed to Shelagh to be generous and reasonable, though the separation from Camillo would be trying, but the interval would give her time to save a little money towards her wedding outfit out of her salary and settle her affairs. But Camillo was furious. Brought up by the indulgent housekeeper, Giovanna, who had presided over the Barsini household since his mother's death, except for the short period of his father's second marriage, he had become thoroughly spoiled. Cesare had been too busy to give much time to his children and it was only of late years that he had had leisure to retire to the Isola di Santa Lucia during the summer months; even then he kept in touch with his various concerns, flying to various parts of Italy for several days at a time, for he was far from being the hermit Camillo had implied.

By the time he was twenty, the harm had been done, and what Camillo desired he expected to acquire without delay. He could see no reason why he should not marry Shelagh then and there without being parted from her. They could honeymoon in the Italian lake district while the house in Genoa was being prepared for them, and he was confident he could take on an executive position without serving even a few months' apprenticeship. Shelagh had no family to consider, no obligations to discharge; anything she needed he could buy for her. It was absurd to let her return to England where he might lose her, though actually he had little fear of that. But Cesare was firm. A few months' probation would be no great hardship and would give them an opportunity to test the durability of their emotions. They could write to each other and he had no objection to Camillo going to England to visit his fiancée occasionally, provided that he did not neglect his business duties. They were both very young and they had only known each other for a matter of days, so to delay was wise because marriage was for always. Cesare did not approve of the recent legislation in Italy to sanction divorce, and most of his countrymen supported him. All of which sounded very sensible, though Shelagh had to suppress an uneasy suspicion that Cesare hoped one or other of them would change their mind during the waiting time. In this she wronged him, as she was to discover in the distant future.

Gillian told her she was a fool to submit to Cesare's

dictation. She should support Camillo, and since they were both of age, they could wed and, faced with an accomplished fact, his formidable father would come round. Her friend's romance seemed to Gillian to be almost too good to be true, and she wanted her to make it irrevocable before obstacles arose.

'Grab him while you can,' she advised.

'You mean you don't think Cam's love will last six months?' Shelagh asked curiously. She herself did not doubt that it would.

'Well, he *is* Italian, and they aren't famed for fidelity,' Gillian pointed out. 'Don't push your luck, Shee. It's such a marvellous Cinderella story I'd hate it to come unstuck.'

'It won't,' Shelagh told her confidently. 'And I've got things to see to before I'm married—working out my notice and finding you another flatmate, to say nothing of buying clothes. I don't want Camillo to have to do that. It's bad enough having to accept the wedding expenses. That's to be in Venice and Signor Barsini footing the bill. In fact he's being so very generous that I feel I must fall in with his wishes.'

'Too generous,' Gillian hinted darkly. 'Mark my words, he'll throw a spanner in the works if he can.'

'I'm sure you misjudge him,' Shelagh insisted, stifling her own uneasiness. Cesare's acquiescence still puzzled her. In vulgar parlance she was no catch for his handsome affluent son, but so long as Camillo stayed true, he had committed himself. Swept along on a high tide of passionate infatuation, she was certain that Camillo was the love of her life, and she of his, and their love would endure ... well, perhaps not for ever, but for many years until it mellowed into mutual understanding and affection to light their advancing years while they brought up the family with which she hoped they would be blessed.

Camillo suddenly capitulated and agreed to his father's terms. He told Shelagh airily that perhaps it would be wiser to fall in with his father's wishes and it would be a shame to antagonise him. She complimented him upon his consideration for his parent, and he gave her a quizzical look, not thinking it necessary to inform her that Cesare had indicated firmly that there would be a shortage of cash if he did not comply. Once he was established and earning a substantial salary he could do as he pleased, but until then his father held the purse strings.

'But mind you behave yourself,' he admonished her. 'If when I come to London I find you have other men, I will kill you.'

'Oh, Cam, don't exaggerate!' Shelagh told him, laughing, though she was thrilled by his Latin jealousy. 'There'll never be anyone but you, don't dare to doubt me.'

The exchange ended in a fervent embrace, and both were reassured of the permanency of their love.

London seemed dull and drab after the Italian sunshine, and Shelagh did not find the prospect of winter with its smog and cold in front of her alluring, but she consoled herself by reflecting that it would be the last one she would spend in England and in planning her wedding outfit. Gillian was to be her bridesmaid and she was to travel out to Italy with her for the wedding. Camillo had decided upon a honeymoon in Paris, when they would shop, and he had told her he meant to buy for her all the expensive clothes that her beauty merited. He had given her a ring, an emerald surrounded by brilliants, which she enjoyed showing off to her workmates, though she was secretly terrified of losing it, for it was very valuable.

She went to visit the convent and the simple nuns were overjoyed by her good fortune.

'You were made for love and marriage,' one of them said to her. 'Though there is no higher vocation than to serve our blessed Lord, you've not the temperament to make a nun. We always knew that.'

Only Mother Cecilia was dubious.

'He knows all about you? You've told him the truth?' she enquired.

'Yes, and he doesn't mind, he declares that it's me he's marrying, not my family,' Shelagh replied happily. 'In fact he seems rather pleased that I haven't got any relations to interfere.'

'But *his* family? Will they receive you with kindness?'

'He's only got a father, and he was ... quite agreeable.'

As she remembered her conversation with Cesare, Shelagh's brows wrinkled. He had been, as she had said, agreeable, but with reservations. There was plenty of time for him to persuade Camillo to change his mind, and though she was certain he would not succeed, she did not believe that he really approved of the marriage.

'Your mother was a housemaid here,' Mother Cecilia said bluntly.

'Yes, I knew that. I told the Barsinis so, they didn't seem to mind.'

Camillo could not care less, nor for her lack of a father, but Cesare, and other Barsini relatives, there must be some, would consider he was making a misalliance. Again she felt a stab of apprehension.

For the first two months after her return Camillo wrote or phoned every day. His letters were extravagantly expressed and sometimes made her blush. Her answers seemed to her to be prim and cool, as she told him, for she could not put her heart on paper. He replied that they pleased him, for they betrayed her innocence and inexperience, but once she belonged to him he would soon change all that. Then he excitedly told her that he was coming to London for a weekend.

They greeted each other rapturously, but the two days of his visit were marred for Shelagh by his importunities. He wanted her to stay with him at his hotel where he had booked a double room.

'You can't have scruples now since we are to be married so soon,' he urged her.

Afterwards, when he had gone back to Italy, Shelagh wondered how she had found the strength to refuse him, but some instinct prompted her to deny him. Later, she thought it must have been her guardian angel watching over her. The nuns believed firmly in such beings. Camillo took her refusal better than she had dared to hope, admitting it was not the custom in his country to anticipate marriage.

In the bleak days following Christmas he wrote infrequently, complaining that he had said all there was to say and what were words on paper when he wanted her warm body in '*mie braccie*'. Also he was being kept 'nose to the grindstone, as you say', at his job and had little time for correspondence.

It was Cesare who informed her about the final arrangements. He had booked rooms for her and Gillian at a hotel in Venice. After the civil wedding and the ceremony in church, which would be attended by a few family friends, they would cross to the Isola di Santa Lucia in a special launch for a meal. Then Camillo would accompany the two girls back to Venice airport, from whence Gillian would fly home and the bridal pair to Paris.

Shelagh had asked if Rita could also be a bridesmaid, but Camillo had objected. She would be a nuisance, he declared, unless there was someone to look after her, which would mean inviting Giovanna or

Miss Barnes—she was always called 'Miss'—neither of whom would grace the occasion. Shelagh deplored his attitude, she would have welcomed all three of them, but thought it wiser not to persist.

On the morning before her departure she received a short note from Camillo in which he informed her that his father would meet her plane. She probably knew that it was not etiquette for them to see each other before the ceremony. It contained none of his usual impassioned phrases and she felt vaguely chilled by its lack of ardour, though he signed himself 'your adoring and impatient lover'.

On the same day, Gillian developed measles, a disaster no one could have foreseen. Shelagh, who had had the complaint and was unlikely to take it again, was sick with disappointment, as also was poor spotty Gillian. Shelagh telegraphed Cesare telling him that she would be alone and contacted Gillian's mother. Luckily Mrs Dawson was able to come to nurse her daughter, while Shelagh completed her packing in low spirits.

She was not going to wear any of the usual bridal trimmings, for the ceremony was to be very quiet. She had chosen a plain white dress in broderie anglaise and a white crinoline hat. Gillian's more elaborate gown in pink chiffon remained hanging in the wardrobe. Venice sounded a romantic place in which to be married and she had an ardent bridegroom awaiting her, but no one of her own would be there; she would be among foreigners and strangers, with only Camillo to support her, and even he was slightly alien. Bitterly did she regret Gillian's unfortunate illness, but there was just nothing to be done about it.

'Camillo will make up for everything,' she told herself feverishly. 'At last we're going to be alone together with no barrier between us.'

Cesare Barsini was waiting for her as she came off the plane. Beautifully groomed and formally dressed in a light suit, he looked very much the distinguished aristocrat among the casually clad tourists. He greeted her with grave courtesy and almost, it seemed to her, commiseration. It must be because Gillian had been unable to come, she decided; he knew she must be feeling isolated and her heart warmed towards him. They crossed the lagoon by boat, Paolo, the Italian sailor who was in charge of it, helping her aboard. Distant Venice, connected to the mainland by its long causeway, lifted its distinctive campanile into an azure sky. A little breeze raised the hair on Shelagh's forehead and she welcomed it after the stuffy cabin of the plane. Her depression was replaced by a feeling of contentment.

'It's good to be back,' she said to Cesare, who sat opposite to her, while Paolo manipulated the controls.

'You like Venezia?'

'Yes. I'm rather sorry I'm to live in Genoa, though I'm sure it's very nice.'

A strange expression crossed Cesare's face, and he looked away from her over the green-blue water. She had a sudden premonition that something was wrong, but all he said was:

'Venezia can be dreary in the winter and Genova is a very fine town. I go there myself for part of the year.'

'So we shall see something of you?'

He did not answer, and her uneasiness grew.

'Cam is all right?' she asked anxiously.

'He is perfectly well, I believe,' Cesare replied guardedly.

They've quarrelled, she thought, I hope not about me. She enquired about Margarita, and was informed she also was well.

'Incidentally, she is waiting to welcome you at your

hotel,' Cesare went on. 'As your friend is sick I decided it would not be correct for you to stay there alone, so Rita and Miss Barnes are occupying her room. I do not think you met Miss Barnes, she was away when you were here before. She is a very estimable lady and has had charge of Rita since she was small, and I hope she will stay with us until the child is old enough to go to boarding school. She is, as you know, a country-woman of your own.'

He seemed relieved to be able to expand about his daughter, a safer topic than his son, evidently.

'You are very thoughtful, *signore*,' she commended him. 'But was it necessary to go to all this trouble for one night?'

'I considered it so,' he said shortly.

Something in his tone frightened her, but she instantly quelled her fear. She was overwrought and nervous, ready to read significance into the most ordinary words, but oh, how she wished Camillo was there to reassure her, though she knew it would be considered unconventional. Surely in these unusual circumstances formality could have been waived? But she dared not suggest it to the austere gentleman sitting opposite to her.

The hotel selected for her sojourn was one of the best in the city, being situated on the waterfront not far from the Piazza San Marco, a long, low building decorated with window boxes and trailing creepers on its outside. Paolo ran the launch expertly alongside the landing stage, and a porter came hurrying out to take her luggage. Cesare handed her out and escorted her into the marble-floored vestibule to the reception desk. She signed the register, handed over her passport and was given her key. Cesare waited beside her and as she turned away, said:

'Your room is on the first floor, Rita and Miss Barnes

are next door, but I have told them not to disturb you until you have bathed and rested. I will have tea sent up to you and we will all dine together.'

They had moved across the vestibule while he was speaking and he indicated a wide stairway with shallow steps up which the porter was carrying her cases. She followed him up the short flight, found her number at the head of it, and the porter unlocked the door. It was a beautiful room, decorated in white and gold its walls hung appropriately with gilt-framed Venetian mirrors, reflecting its interior in endless duplication. The windows looked out over the water and an open door revealed an adjoining bedroom. She had been provided with a suite! The porter put down her cases and she fumbled in her purse for a coin, but found Cesare had followed her and he forestalled her. She caught an oddly compassionate gleam in the porter's liquid dark eyes. Pity for the bride, for of course the staff would know all about her, but how strange! Perhaps since Italians made so much of family he was sorry that she had no one with her. Cesare gave the man some instruction in Italian, and as he disappeared, said to her:

'You will be comfortable here, *sí*? There is a *bagno* connected with the *camera*.'

'It's luxurious!' she exclaimed.

'*Bene*. Before we dine I would speak with you. I will return at...' He consulted his watch and named a time. 'Ah, here is your tea.'

A waiter knocked on the half open door and came in bearing a tray, which he set on a table in front of the window.

'I will leave you for the present,' Cesare said as the man withdrew.

'One moment, *signore*,' Shelagh intercepted him. 'Is

Camillo in Venice? I ... I should like to ring him. I suppose you've no objection?'

For then her vague fears would be laid to rest and she had a sudden intense desire to hear Camillo's voice.

'I'm afraid that is not possible,' Cesare returned. 'I have no objection, but at the moment I do not know where he is staying. He has not informed me.'

Shelagh stared at him. 'But ... but tomorrow?'

'Is tomorrow.' He gazed up at the ornately decorated ceiling. 'This is Camillo's last night of freedom; he celebrates.'

'Oh yes.' Camillo would be preparing to enjoy the Italian equivalent of a stag party and would not welcome feminine intervention, even hers. All the same, he might have rung up or left a message to welcome her upon arrival.

'*Ciao*,' Cesare said, and left her.

Shelagh sat down on a comfortable chair by the window and poured out a cup of tea. A sunblind shaded the window, beyond which the sunlight simmered on the water. Every sort of craft was passing, high-powered black gondolas, *vaporetti*, sailing ships and motor launches, and in the distance the white bulk of a cruise liner gliding out of the Canale della Giudecca. Cesare had something to tell her and she surmised it was connected with his son. Had their plans had to be altered? Perhaps their honeymoon was postponed due to press of business, or Camillo had proved inefficient at his work and Cesare was about to suggest some alternative. A daunting thought. Knowing her fiancé's temperament the last seemed to be quite probable, and naturally Cesare would be disappointed. Possibly he wanted to discuss with her his new ideas for their future. Well, she would know in good time, and meanwhile her head was aching and she would like to lie down.

The bed was wide and soft, and as soon as she subsided upon it, Shelagh fell asleep. She woke to discover the sunset was painting the sky with rainbow hues and she had slept for two hours. That did not matter as Cesare was not yet due and she had time to shower and change. She felt rested and ready to face whatever unpleasant disclosures he was going to make.

She took off the trouser suit in which she had travelled and put on an evening dress, one of the two she had brought with her, a wispy affair in black chiffon trimmed with silver that packed easily. It had a square neckline and full transparent sleeves gathered into a cuff. She had lost her summer tan and her white arms and shoulders gleamed through the thin material. Her long hair waved naturally and she brushed it until it shone like guinea-gold. She applied make-up to her too pale cheeks and green eye-shadow to bring out the colour of her eyes. The faint bruises under them, the result of fatigue, only made them look larger and slightly mysterious. With Camillo's ring upon her finger and a necklace of jade she considered she looked quite presentable enough to grace Cesare's swagger hotel. She gave a little sigh. If only Camillo were going to be there she would look forward to the evening.

A knock on the outer door must be Cesare. Shelagh called out, 'Come in' and went to meet him in her sitting room. It was dark until he switched on the light and she saw he was wearing a white jacket with dark trousers, his olive face as smooth as marble, his hair black as a crow's wing, shining as if polished. A sudden gleam lit his grey eyes as he beheld her.

'But you are beautiful, Sancia.'

She winced. Nobody called her that except Camillo, who was not present. Hastily she corrected him.

'Please, my name is Shelagh.'

'Shelagh! Is that right?'

She said it was and he repeated it.

'It sounds enchanting.'

She looked at him uneasily. He was wasting time paying her empty compliments. Her name was of no interest to him.

'You've something you want to say to me?'

'Something I *have* to say to you,' he amended. 'It is, I fear, unpleasant.' He paused, seemingly uncertain how to proceed, but his disclosure, whatever it was, had to be postponed, for as once before she had interrupted them, Rita came flying into the room in a whirl of pale blue flounces.

'*Signorina* ... Shelagh, you see Miss Barnes teach me to say your name. You have come and now we all have *pranzo* together. Me, I am all excitement!'

'So I see,' her father said sternly. 'Rita, Rita, where are your manners? Bursting in without kocking upon the door.' He frowned ferociously. 'I shall send you to bed at once.'

'Ah no, Papa, please.' But he did not mean it, as she knew very well. Shelagh, not so sure, hastened to say:

'Please forgive her. Her crime is her eagerness to see me, and I find that flattering. What a pretty frock, Rita.'

Rita spread her flounced skirts and pirouetted round the room.

'It is for the *festa* ... party after the wedding when you come to the Isola. Miss Barnes says it is too ... too elaborate.' She spread the long word out syllable by syllable, 'but Papa says it is *bella* and I may have it.'

Cesare's face had darkened and he seemed about to speak, then altered what he had been going to say.

'*Bene*, shall we have dinner?' he proposed. 'Shelagh, we will have to talk later when this disturber of the peace has gone to bed. *Scusi,* I have to speak to Miss Barnes.'

He left the room and Rita ran to Shelagh, flinging her arms about her neck.

'I am so glad to see you again!'

'Careful!' Shelagh warned. 'I'm tidied up for dinner and so are you.' She kissed the child's velvet cheek and smiled at her as she disengaged herself. Rita regarded her with her head on one side.

'You are much too nice for Camillo,' she declared. 'Why do you not marry Papa? He is much better.'

Shelagh laughed and flushed. 'He hasn't asked me,' she said lightly. 'Your brother did.'

'You mean he got in first,' Rita suggested. Her English had improved since Shelagh had last seen her and was a curious mixture of colloquial phrases and mixed grammar. 'Everyone says I need a *mamma,*' the child went on gaily. 'And you'd make me a super one. Why didn't you wait?'

'Because I fell in love with Camillo,' Shelagh told her, thinking young Margarita was something of an *infant terrible.* Vaguely she wondered if Cesare had ever contemplated marrying again. 'Cam's nearer my age,' she pointed out.

'*Sciocchezze!*' Rita waved a contemptuous hand. 'There was Signore Orsini, he marry a girl half his age.' Her eyes narrowed wickedly. 'He is very rich, everybody say she is very lucky. Papa has lots of money too.'

'I'm afraid you listen to gossip that isn't meant for little girls,' Shelagh told her severely.

'Oh, I listen to everything,' Rita announced. 'How else can I come to know what goes on?'

Cesare returned escorting Miss Barnes, a youngish woman with faded brown hair and spectacles covering pale blue eyes. He introduced her to Shelagh, whom she eyed furtively, and they went down to dinner.

The restaurant was a lovely room with windows wide open on to a balcony overhanging the water and illuminated with chandeliers dropping crystal pendants from the ceiling. Shelagh's surroundings were not lacking in glamour. The room was filled with a cosmopolitan crowd speaking different languages. Rita was very excited and chattered volubly throughout the meal. As with most Italian children she usually sat up for dinner, but dinner at a hotel was an unaccustomed treat. Miss Barnes was quietly dignified and seldom spoke. Shelagh learned from the few questions she was able to put to her that she had had several positions abroad and had often found herself in strange company, but her manner towards the bride was constrained and the one subject uppermost in all their minds, the wedding on the morrow, was not mentioned, nor did anyone speak of Camillo. Shelagh caught Miss Barnes eyeing her with watery sympathy, and she began to believe that some disaster had befallen her fiancé, and they did not know how to break the news to her. Rita had not been told, but the hotel staff, the governess and Cesare knew. He had been about to tell her when his daughter had come in upon them and he had decided she had better have her dinner first.

With her increasing anxiety, her appetite left her. She refused the delectable ice pudding that Rita hailed with glee and waited on tenterhooks for them to finish. Cesare was watching her with concern and pressed her to drink more wine as if he wished to fortify her for the disclosure he would have to make. At length, unable to contain herself any longer, she whispered to him:

'Something's happened to Camillo, hasn't it?'

She was startled by the effect her question had upon

her host. Cesare's urbane manner vanished, his black brows drew together over eyes that smouldered, as he returned shortly:

'I very much regret to have to tell you that nothing has.'

There was such venom in his quiet voice that Shelagh was appalled; wildly she conjectured what Camillo could have done to produce such a reaction; absconding with money entrusted to him seemed the most likely, but surely Camillo could not be a thief?

'Something is wrong?' she faltered.

Cesare raised a long-fingered hand to stop her from probing further. 'Presently,' he murmured.

For Shelagh all glamour had faded from the scene, the lights seemed garish and swam before her tired eyes, the indifferent gaily chattering tourists at the other tables became an irritation. Her pallor was noticeable under her make-up, and the shadows under her eyes became more pronounced.

'Signorina Riordan is very tired,' Cesare broke in upon Rita's lively discourse; his gaze rested upon her with evident concern.

Miss Barnes, practised in sensing her employers' moods, said to her charge:

'If you've finished, little one, it's time you were in bed,' and half rose from her seat.

Rita began to protest, she wanted another peach and she was loth to end her enchanted evening, but her father told her sharply:

'Take it with you, your governess is right, it is past your bedtime.' He rose from his seat and pushed back his chair. 'You would like coffee, Miss Barnes, *si*? It shall be sent up to your room.'

His courtesy towards a dependant touched Shelagh in spite of her woe. In the midst of a family crisis he ensured that the governess should not be deprived of her after-dinner coffee. Alice Barnes's dim blue eyes were worshipping as she said goodnight to him.

Shelagh kissed Rita and wished her a happy awakening.

'And you too, it is your great day,' Rita said, whereat her elders exchanged significant glances. The child followed in the wake of her governess clutching a peach.

Cesare watched them go and waved to Rita as she looked back when she reached the doorway. Then he turned to Shelagh.

'Shall we go to the privacy of your *salotto*?' he asked quietly.

He beckoned to a hovering waiter and ordered coffee and cognac to be brought up to them, also Miss Barnes's coffee to be served in her room.

Shelagh rose to her feet, still cogitating upon what crime Camillo could have committed to so affect his father, for apparently he was not ill or physically harmed. Embezzlement and forgery flickered through her mind, but surely he had no need to do anything like that? His brief note of the day before had given no hint of catastrophe, so whatever had occurred must have happened very suddenly. Cesare took her arm and guided her out of the restaurant, their fellow diners giving them a cursory glance as they passed. The tall man was impressive, the girl had wonderful hair, then they dismissed them and continued with their discussion of the day's trivial doings, while a waiter hastened to clear the table at which they had sat ready for further occupants.

CHAPTER FOUR

CESARE flicked on the light as they entered Shelagh's suite, illuminating the room in all its baroque grandeur. Outside some amorous youth was strumming a guitar, his clear tenor audible above the other sounds singing an Italian love song. *Amore Mia* quivered on the air in tender tones. Cesare muttered an imprecation and strode across the floor to close the windows, excluding the sentimental ditty. Shelagh sat down in the chair she had previously occupied; she had lost all sense of reality and felt that she was moving in a dream. The mirrors on the walls reflected an endless repetition of dark elegant men and bright-haired girls, increasing the sense of fantasy. Soon she would wake and discover she had fallen asleep in the plane and none of this evening's bizarre events had happened.

Cesare came to stand opposite to her looking down at her with an expression that in someone she knew better she would have described as tender—but that was ridiculous as applied to him. He could only regard her as a nuisance that Camillo's fickleness had inflicted upon him, for she had an increasing certainty of what he was going to tell her. It could be the only possible explanation of his evasions.

'I am afraid I am about to give you a nasty shock,' he said gently, thinking how slight and vulnerable she looked huddled in the capacious chair. Some premonition must have prompted her to wear black; she looked like a desolate young widow before she had been a wife. 'I wish I could spare you,' he went on, 'but there is only one thing I can do to help you, and that solution may not appeal to you.'

'Please let me have it in plain English,' she said wearily. 'Are you trying to tell me that Cam has walked out on me?'

A discreet knock delayed his answer. It was the waiter bringing in the coffee and cognac. In silence they watched him set the tray on a small table which he drew up in front of Shelagh. Cesare tipped him and the man wished them '*Buona notte*' with a white-toothed conspiratorial grin. He believes we're going to sleep together, Shelagh thought, and shivered at the bare idea. Cesare was as awe-inspiring as that other Cesare—Cesare Borgia—and she was sure he could be as ruthless as any of that notorious clan, who did not scruple to use poison to remove those who stood in their way. Fascinated, her eyes searched his unrevealing face, while she waited for his confirmation. If Camillo had repudiated her she was sure his father had manoeuvred him.

The waiter closed the door noiselessly behind him and Cesare proceeded to pour out the coffee without speaking.

'Well, are you?' she demanded impatiently.

He threw her a brief flickering glance.

'He has run away,' he said baldly.

Shelagh moistened her lips with the tip of her tongue. Ever since she had landed at the airport she had been aware of an atmosphere, and it emanated from the man standing before her coolly manipulating the coffee. She could not believe that Camillo would voluntarily desert her. He had been forced to depart due to the machinations of this domineering aristocrat who considered she was unworthy to be his wife. From the moment he had met her he had been playing her as a fisherman plays a fish before he delivered the fatal blow. The luxury of the hotel, the dinner, Rita's presence had all been contrived to lull her into acceptance of a situation which he had deliberately engineered while he plied her with false sympathy. She had always suspected that Cesare secretly opposed the marriage.

Her green eyes sparkled irefully as she accused him. 'You mean you've driven him away?'

'Dio mio!' Cesare exploded. 'Are you out of your mind? I have done everything within my power to keep him here, but he has taken fright. He confessed to me that marriage and its responsibilities were more than he could take upon his shoulders. I could have wrung his neck!'

'I don't believe you,' Shelagh said flatly. 'I received a letter from him just before I left telling me you would be meeting me as it was not correct for him to do so, but there was no hint that he wouldn't be here.' (But it had been a cold little note and it had chilled her.) 'That was yesterday, *signore*, and it makes nonsense of your assertion that he had fled. Camillo would never willingly leave me in the lurch. You've spirited him away.' Her voice rose stridently as anger and suppressed fear overwhelmed her. She sprang to her feet, glaring at Cesare over the coffee table. 'You never wanted him to marry me, did you? A penniless, nameless nobody, though you'd have been more honest if you'd said so. But you hoped he'd tire of me, that our love would die a natural death, saving you trouble. When it didn't you ... what have you done with him? Kidnapped him?'

She looked magnificent, her eyes glittering, her hair a burnished mass on her shoulders, her body taut as a drawn bowstring. Cesare's grey eyes kindled in response, but he rebuked her calmly.

'Compose yourself, little spitfire. You are talking nonsense...'

'Am I?' She moved round the table towards him, her fists clenched. 'I believe you're capable of any wickedness to get your own way. What have you done with Cam? I demand to know, I must know!' She clutched at the lapels of his jacket, her body trembling, her eyes green wells of anguish in her white face. 'Tell me, you inhuman brute, tell me!'

His hands closed round her wrists like steel fetters, holding her away from him.

'*Basta, piccolina,* you are hysterical.'

'Can you wonder?' she cried desperately. 'That you could do this to us!'

With strong ungentle hands he forced her back into her chair.

'Sit down and listen to reason.'

'I won't... I can't...'

Her mixed emotions combined with fatigue swept over her in a storm of tears, she began to sob wildly.

'You will,' Cesare told her. Very deliberately he slapped her face. The blow checked her weeping as nothing else would have done, and slowly she regained control of herself and her sobs subsided. Wiping her eyes with a wisp of handkerchief, she said bitterly:

'Was that the act of a gentleman?'

'It is my method of dealing with an overwrought woman. Harsh perhaps, but effective. Now, drink some coffee and then perhaps you will allow me to speak.'

Shelagh flashed him a rebellious look, but she took a sip of the coffee he was holding to her lips. It was laced with cognac and the spirit coursing through her veins steadied her. A numb despair replaced her former rage. She was helpless and at Cesare's mercy since Camillo had either willingly or unwillingly abandoned her. Cesare said:

'I would not lie to you, Shelagh, I assure you. I had no intention of trying to part you two. Birth and dowries are of no account weighed against loyalty and honesty. Having had a wide experience of women ...' he smiled wryly, '... I think I gauged your character correctly. You are the sort of girl I wanted for my son, and it is Camillo who has proved unworthy. So control that waspish tongue of yours, I do not deserve its sting.'

He spoke so simply and sincerely that Shelagh became convinced that her accusations had been groundless. He had told her the truth and had had nothing to do with Camillo's desertion. Mutely she stared up into his stern face and saw compassion in his eyes which stung her unbearably. She had been abandoned and rejected and he was pitying her plight, despising her perhaps for falling for Camillo's facile charms. He had told her once she was not the first girl with whom his son had been in love. She gave a long sigh and turned her head away as her lovely dream of marital happiness faded before the breath of harsh reality. It had been too ephemeral to last. Clutching at the remnants of her pride, she said quietly:

'I apologise. I shouldn't have spoken as I did. You've been very forbearing.' She smiled wanly. 'I was abusing the wrong man.'

'You were,' he returned uncompromisingly. 'An inhuman brute!' He shook his head. 'You do not mince your words, young woman.'

'I ... I'm sorry.'

'*Va bene.* Believe me, I wish to be your friend.'

'I don't see how you can be in the circumstances,' Shelagh remarked. She drank some more coffee and was able to face him with composure. 'It was all a dreadful mistake, wasn't it?' she went on sadly. 'We ...

we weren't suited and I should never have taken him seriously, but...'

'You had every reason to take him seriously,' Cesare cut in. 'The young blackguard was determined to marry you until he began to realise that marriage would clip his wings.' He started to pace the room with long strides and the reflections in the mirrors recorded his movements in a procession of black and white figures. 'The trouble I have had with that boy,' he exclaimed. 'Gambling, debts, women ... but I excused him on account of his youth. The Barsini have always been a little wild in adolescence, but made good citizens when they reached manhood. I fear Camillo inherited an irresponsible temperament from his mother. I hoped his feeling for you was genuine and he would settle down under your guidance, and his marriage might be the making of him. I wanted him to have every chance.' He ceased his prowling and smiled ruefully at Shelagh. 'You see, I too had illusions, but I should have known it was hopeless and I should have warned you he was not reliable.'

'I wouldn't have listened to anything against him,' Shelagh returned. 'To me he was a sort of young prince and I was infatuated.' Her face became infinitely sad. 'I'd never met anyone like him before and it seemed a miracle that he loved me, only it wasn't really love, was it?'

Cesare shrugged his shoulders. 'I could call it a less pretty name.' His grey eyes swept over the girl's slight figure. 'You are a very desirable woman, *mia cara*.'

'Ah no!' Shelagh shrank from the sudden glint in his eyes. 'I'm only a credulous fool. But when did Cam go? Couldn't you have stopped me from coming here?'

'How?' Cesare demanded sardonically. 'Sent you a telegram saying "Bridegroom absconded"? That would have been very cruel. Actually though I knew he was wavering I thought I had persuaded him to stay, until last night I received a note from him saying he had left Venice and would not return. He did not write to you?'

'Yes, I told you, but he only explained why he couldn't meet me himself.'

'*Madonna mia*, the cowardly swine!' Cesare exclaimed forcibly. 'He had not even the courage to tell you the truth!' Mastering his anger, he went on gently: 'I decided it was best you should come here so that I could explain the whole miserable situation to you in person and if possible make amends.'

'A nice thought,' Shelagh told him. 'But there's nothing you can do.'

'You have been deserted and insulted!'

She winced. 'Don't please rub it in. All that you can do for me now is to send me home. Oh...!' Her hand flew to her mouth. She had no home, no job to which she could return. She had given up her position and Gillian had another flatmate arriving, when she had recovered from her measles. The convent would always welcome her, but she shrank from the nuns' pitying concern.

Cesare seemed to have guessed her thoughts, for he said:

'You have no home, have you? Nor a family to support you and offer solace in your distress. That makes Camillo's conduct all the more reprehensible. I can at least offer you a refuge. The Isola di Santa Lucia is a good place in which to heal a broken heart.'

'You're very kind.' She recalled that Cesare had lost two wives. He had apparently not grieved much for the first one, but he had never spoken of Rita's mother. That perhaps had been a brief idyll and it was for her he mourned in his island retreat. But she had no wish to seek solace there herself. Italy was too full of memories of her lost love.

'I'd rather return to England,' she decided. A sudden gleam of hope illuminated her features. '*Signore*, is it possible Camillo may get over his cold feet and ... and come back to me?'

Anger flashed in Cesare's grey eyes. 'I would not have him back, and if you have any pride neither would you.'

She dropped her head. 'Love is stronger than pride.'

'It is too late. I have disowned him.'

Shelagh threw a startled glance at his implacable face.

'Isn't that rather too drastic?' she faltered. 'Your only son?'

He hesitated. 'You had better hear it all,' he said finally. 'Then you will cherish no false hopes. He has flown to America, and he has not gone alone.'

It wanted only that to complete her humiliation.

'Another girl?' she asked tonelessly.

'Hardly a girl, a wealthy American. She was spending the winter in Italy and he neglected his work to be with her. That was after he returned from seeing you in London. I warned him I would not countenance such behaviour when he was affianced to you. He promised he would break with her, but he did not. Then I discovered he was accepting money from her. *Dio mio*, that a son of mine could allow himself to be kept by a woman!'

Shelagh gave a long sigh. That was why Camillo's letters had become short and infrequent. Her disillusionment was now complete.

'I must go back tomorrow,' she said desolately, recoiling from the thought of meeting Gillain and her other friends.

'That will not be very pleasant for you.'

She laughed forcedly. 'Jilted at the altar, so to speak. No, it won't be very pleasant, but I'll survive.'

She made a pitiful attempt at bravado, but she looked forlorn and vulnerable.

'There is no need for you to be jilted at all,' Cesare said.

She stared at him in puzzled bewilderment. 'You mean you've been hoaxing me? Camillo will come back?'

Cesare's stern face softened as he said very gently:

'No, *piccolina,* he will never come back, but I do not wish you to have to return to your friends with your pride in the dust. If you could bring yourself to accept me in my son's stead there can be a wedding after all.'

Now surely the shock of Camillo's perfidy had addled her wits. Cesare could not have really made such a suggestion. Dumbly she gazed up at his dark patrician face in which the grey eyes were so unexpected. They should have been black and velvety like Cam's. Camillo! She must accept that she would never see him again. She became aware that Cesare was still speaking.

'Rita needs a mother and she likes you. I know I must seem old to you, a poor substitute for my son, but at least I can offer you a home and protection. You need not go back a deserted bride.' He smiled with winning sweetness. 'You will be the Isola's honoured mistress. Is not that a little compensation for your loss?'

'You can't really mean it,' she blurted out, adding childishly: 'We're not in love.'

His face became hard as marble. 'I think you have learned how unreliable so-called love can be.'

She winced. 'I have, but oh, *signore . . .*'

'Cesare,' he interrupted, 'you must call me that.'

'I can't . . . I mean, it's presumptuous. You're a great gentleman.'

'Which my son was not?' He lifted his head arrogantly. 'The honour of my house demands that I should make you full recompense.'

Shelagh drew her hand over her brows. She must be dreaming, for his proposition was utterly fantastic, and surely nobody bothered about family honour nowadays? It was not a good reason for a loveless marriage with a man old enough to be her father who was practically a stranger to her, and an intimidating one at that. Yet his offer, if he did really mean it, was enormously attractive, for it would preclude the necessity of returning to London to face the barrage of her friends' pity and contempt—contempt because she had allowed herself to be so easily beguiled. Even Gillian had been secretly a little jealous of her romance and would not be altogether sorry that it had ended so tragically. But surely there was an easier way than the drastic one of marriage to serve his purpose if his object was to provide a companion for Rita. She broke the long silence by saying:

'If you are thinking about Rita, couldn't I be her governess or something? I mean, I hardly aspire to be your . . . your wife.'

'Rita already has a competent governess,' he returned, watching the varying emotions chase over her mobile features. That she had not immediately leaped at his offer was a mark in her favour. It showed she was not mercenary. 'Nor will she require one much longer,' he went on. 'I said she needed a mother, a woman who will be permanent in her life. I do not wish her to go the same way as Camillo. I also need a hostess when I entertain, as I do when I go to Genova . . .' Shelagh made an inarticulate sound and he paused. 'You feel you would be inadequate?'

'Very much so.'

'You are young enough to learn. You can be trained for what I shall require of you,' a suggestion which Shelagh did not altogether relish. She thought Cesare could be a hard taskmaster, and suppose she failed him?

'You are not stupid,' he went on, 'and you are quite beautiful. You would look very ornamental at the head of my dinner table.'

She blushed under his appraising regard, and said wryly:

'You like red hair?'

'It is a glorious colour. You will look like a Venetian duchess, properly dressed, of course.'

'Oh!' Her blush deepened, as did her discomfort. He made her feel like a slave up for auction—so much white flesh, so much red hair to titillate his friends' appreciation of his new possession. He would dress her and pamper her, and in return ... she turned her head away ... there was a physical side to marriage; could she endure that?

He continued persuasively: '*Ecco*, you shall have every luxury, for as you know I am not a poor man, and I will settle money upon you so that whatever happens you will have provision for the future. Is it not worth your consideration?'

'You're more than generous, but ... but ...' She stared uneasily round the beautiful room, at the mirrors endlessly reflecting their two figures, the handsome aristocratic man and her humble self, such an incongruous pair. It was his natural setting, but not hers. Meeting Cesare's intent gaze, she blushed again and nervously pleated the stuff of her skirt between her fingers while her heart began to beat suffocatingly fast.

'*Signore*, you overwhelm me,' she murmured. Then

lifting her head she raised frightened eyes to his. 'I don't think ... I can perform ... a wife's duties.'

She wondered if he had understood her, and apparently he had, for his well-shaped mouth twisted in a wry smile as he said:

'*Piccolina,* I shall not ask them of you. I told you all I require is a mother for my daughter and a hostess for my table.'

His words were reassuring though uncomplimentary to her womanhood. In spite of his gallant remarks, he did not himself desire her, considering her only as a superior sort of nursemaid for Rita and a figurehead when he entertained. It was a cold prospect after Camillo's ardent wooing, but she had learned the worthlessness of that; a bright bubble quickly burst leaving only shreds behind. She was thankful Cesare did not find it necessary to simulate a lover-like approach to her, which would have caused her to refuse him at once. Yet he was still a vigorous man and it was many years since Rita's mother had died, as Camillo had told her. The Isola had revealed no glamorous mistress, for neither the ageing Giovanna nor the plain Miss Barnes could be considered in that role. Surely there must be a woman in his life, and if there were, was that why he was advocating a marriage in name only? He did not need a wife to fulfil his physical needs. She found the thought strangely unpalatable, but it was not a thing about which she could question him.

'I love Rita already,' she told him, and it occurred to her that the child could be a great consolation to her; then to remove the possibility of any misunderstanding, she added: 'I shall never love another man.'

'Camillo is not worthy of such constancy,' Cesare declared.

She had not meant that she would stay faithful to

Camillo's memory, but that after such a shattering disillusionment she would never allow herself to fall in love again, in fact love where men were concerned would always be suspect, but she did not try to explain this to Cesare. If he thought she would always be inconsolable so much the better, it would create a barrier between them if they ever threatened to become emotionally involved. Involved? Why should she think of that? She might in time come to regard him with a mild affection, and he would never consider someone as naïve and inexperienced as herself as other than an elder daughter and quite incapable of giving him the satisfaction the other woman did. Already Cesare's imaginary mistress had become a personality in her mind.

She became aware that Cesare was watching her closely and she coloured faintly, thankful that he could not read her mind. He must be supposing that she was weighing up the pros and cons of his proposition while actually her thoughts had been wandering along irrelevant paths. He said kindly:

'It would be best if you sleep upon it. You must be more than weary after so much travail. Tomorrow I must explain what has happened to Rita. I do not know how she will react to her brother's flight and the postponement of the wedding.'

Shelagh noticed he said postponed, he must be very sure of her, but she made no demur. Instead she observed:

'She doesn't appear to be very fond of him.'

'He gives her no reason to be,' Cesare said drily. 'Unfortunately he has always been jealous of her. He likes to be ... what do you say ... the only pebble on the beach. He resented my marriage to Carlotta, and she did not live long enough to win his affection as I had hoped.'

His face set in a brooding mask and he seemed to forget Shelagh's presence. So he *had* loved his second wife and still mourned her loss, a greater one than she herself had suffered.

'Rita has already told me that she considers you would be a better proposition than her brother,' she informed him, and was surprised that she was able to speak so lightly.

Cesare's frown vanished and he laughed.

'She did? The little minx! *Bene,* I hope you will not disappoint us both.'

'But if I accept you might come to bitterly regret your ... your kindness,' she said anxiously.

'That would be impossible,' he declared gallantly. 'And I shall endeavour to ensure that you never do.'

Flowery phrases, but had they any real meaning?

He came up to her and took her hand between both of his.

'I am not the ogre you seem inclined to think I am,' he told her, 'I will be good to you, *piccolina,* and I will never ask you for what you cannot freely give.'

The clasp of his long nervous fingers sent a quiver down her spine and made her nerves tingle. She became conscious that he was a much more forceful man than his son and possessed of a strong physical magnetism. Involuntarily it occurred to her that if ever he made demands upon her she would find him hard to resist ... if she wanted to resist. Her sensations shocked her; she believed she had become impervious to sex, and surely she could not be so fickle as to find another man attractive so soon after Camillo's desertion? She did not realise that Camillo had aroused her emotions without satisfying them and her young blood was easily stirred; also she had not seen Camillo for some months.

But there was nothing sensual in Cesare's attitude,

no suggestion of amorousness in the way he held her hand, only a wish to reassure her, and her momentary disturbance subsided.

'Goodnight, *cara,*' he said softly. 'Would you like me to obtain for you a sleeping pill?'

She shook her head. 'No, I shan't need it.'

She would not lie awake, for already her decision had been made. The cognac in her coffee must have been potent, for as she glanced over her shoulder to avoid Cesare's too penetrating gaze, their reflections in the mirrors seemed to waver and blur, black hair merging with red-gold locks as they never would in life. A surge of panic washed over her. There was one point about which she must be absolutely certain, that stirring of her pulses when Cesare touched her had shaken her badly. She cried almost incoherently:

'You do understand ... I can't ever love another man, however good he is to me.'

'I thought we had covered that,' Cesare returned patiently. 'Naturally I have accepted that you will never love again.'

There was a mocking twist to his handsome mouth that she failed to notice, and an ironic gleam in his veiled eyes as he lowered his lashes. Cesare was too experienced to take seriously such an assertion from a girl of twenty.

'So long as you know...' Shelagh murmured, uncertain what she was combating; her own weakness or his charisma.

'Believe me, I understand you very well,' Cesare said enigmatically. He released her hand which he seemed to have held for an unnecessarily long time. '*Buona notte, cara,* you will have to learn Italian, you know. *Arrivederci.*'

He made a slight bow.

'Goodnight, *sig* ... Cesare,' she returned mechanically, while it struck her that he was very sure of her answer, also that to learn the language would be the least of her problems.

When he had gone she turned to stare at her image in the mirror. White-faced, wild-eyed, her hair in disorder, she decided that she looked like a scared cat. She could not possibly have appeared tempting to a man like Cesare Barsini who could take his pick of all the smart sophisticated women in Northern Italy, and his sense of chivalry must be very strong to prompt him to make his offer. As far as she could see this marriage of convenience would be far more advantageous to her than to him, and she could bless the family pride and Rita's partiality for her that had been the reasons for his proposal. But it was neither affection for the child nor the profit to be gained that had been the deciding factor. What she could not stomach was the thought of facing Gillian's criticism of her mismanagement of her love affair, and her friend's scornful 'I told you so.'

CHAPTER FIVE

THE succession of emotional shocks Shelagh had sustained drained her vitality and numbed her feelings, so that she sank into a state of apathy in which nothing seemed to matter.

Mechanically she walked through the twin ceremonies that made her Cesare's wife, which had the unreality of a dream, without absorbing their deeper implications. The tall, distinguished man, and Cesare was tall for an Italian, who accompanied her was a stranger to her, and a stranger he remained, for true to his promise he claimed none of a husband's privileges. He treated her much the same as he did his daughter, so that she often forgot that she was Shelagh Barsini and titular mistress of the Casa, for Giovanna continued to run the house and Miss Barnes supervised Margarita's education; in addition to which she had been sent back to school.

Cesare insisted that she must learn Italian thoroughly, and an ancient professor came out from Venice daily to teach her. Her lessons were arranged to coincide with Rita's, but were given in another room. Shelagh soon picked up the conversational phrases, but had difficulty with the intricate grammar. There seemed to be an appalling number of irregular verbs which she must learn before she could attempt to write the language correctly, nor was it very consoling to discover that each district spoke a different dialect. Cesare also wished her to be familiar with Italian history and art. Italy, he said, and in particular Florence, had been the cradle of the Renaissance, or, as he called it the Rinascimento, that extraordinary period when a new interest was kindled in the cultural achievements of ancient Greece, resulting in a flowing of art and literature which slowly seeped through to the rest of Europe. He chose books for her to read dealing with Michelangelo, Canaletto, Petrarch, Dante, Leonardo da Vinci and other famous Italians, but the confusion of continual warfare between the city states, popes and emperors remained a tangle she could never unravel.

'Why must I bother with all this stuff?' she asked Cesare petulantly, thinking he was more like a schoolmaster than a husband.

'Because you will never understand Italy unless you know her history,' he told her firmly.

'But is it necessary that I should?'

'Yes, because you must appear to be a cultivated woman and take an intelligent interest in current affairs when you go into society.'

It was one of the few occasions upon which he had reminded her of her position as his wife, and she stared at him in dismay.

'I don't think I'll be much of a success socially.'

'Persevere, *mia cara*, I am sure you will be adequate when the time comes.'

She felt suddenly cold. 'When we go to Genoa?'

'*Si*. As you know, the island is only a summer residence, but do not agitate yourself, enjoy the sunshine and leave the future to take care of itself.'

She was only too willing to take this advice and once the morning lessons were over, she had the rest of the long hot days to indulge the languor that sapped her energies.

She swam with Rita either in the pool or in the Casa's private lido on the lagoon. Paolo was at their service if his master did not require him and would take them by boat to Venice or any of the other islands if they wished to go. In the evenings they dined late and dressed formally for the meal, and Miss Barnes was promoted to eat with them. This was the only time that Shelagh could count upon seeing her husband, for he was occupied with his own affairs during the day and never took breakfast with them. She did not altogether enjoy his company, for he insisted that they all spoke Italian to give her practice, and often catechised the two girls upon what they had studied during the day. Rita had no awe of him and chattered gaily, but Shelagh felt constrained. Often she would find he was watching her with a look in his eyes that she could not interpret, and she feared he was disappointed by her lack of progress both in learning and sophistication He was often away all day and sometimes all night, but he never told her what he did or where he went. The rest of the household were used to his ways and took them for granted, so she did not like to ask questions, nor did it seem to occur to him that she had a right to be interested in his doings.

In the early morning he often played a set of tennis with Paolo, to keep himself fit, he told Rita, and Shelagh would wake to the sound of balls bouncing off the hard court. Once she went to a window which gave a view of that side of the house and watched the two lithe bronze figures in shorts and singlets engaged in a hard-hitting battle. Cesare looked as lean and agile as his opponent, for the exercise seemed to strip his years from him; he was alert and eager as he smashed down Paolo's services, his dark hair ruffled boyishly about his brow. For the first time he reminded Shelagh of his son and caused her heart to ache. She never watched them again.

Giovanna was friendly and eager to talk, and though Shelagh had qualms about gossiping with a servant she could not restrain her curiosity when the housekeeper dilated upon the subject of her predecessor. After all, since Cesare was so unrevealing about himself, he could not blame her if she sought information elsewhere. She was told that Cesare's marriage to Carlotta d'Este had been the great event of Giovanna's life, for she had been a great lady, descended from the Dukes of Ferrara, and had brought *il signore* a fabulous dowry. The marriage was solemnised in St Mark's in Venice and the celebrations included processions of gondolas taking the guests, who included representatives from all the best families in Italy, to a huge banquet in one of the ancient *palazzos,* which she had been permitted to view from a balcony.

'Era stato magnifico,' Giovanna declared, rolling her eyes.

'Was ... the bride ... very beautiful?' Shelagh asked tentatively.

Giovanna pinched her lip consideringly. 'A poor thing,' she pronounced. 'Sickly from the start. She did not live long after the *bambina* was born. *Il maestro,* he wanted more sons ...' she shrugged her shoulders. 'She was not built to be a good breeder.' She ran a critical eye over Shelagh as if assessing her potentialities for motherhood, and the girl felt her colour rise. Giovanna could be blunt, but she did not know that the connecting door between her bedroom and Cesare's was always locked.

These disclosures indicated that Shelagh had been wrong when she had imagined that Cesare had been madly in love with Carlotta. He had married her for her name and her dowry, and after the failure of his first boyish passion which he had described to her when he was dubious about her infatuation for Camillo, he had become cynical and opted for a great alliance. It was the way of his world where men sought love or what passed for love outside marriage, but did not consider it a necessary ingredient in a legal union. She was strengthened in her conviction that he had a mistress somewhere to console him for two such disasters, and it would seem he visited her on the nights when he was away from the island. Not that it was any concern of hers since she had told him she could never love him, and he had promised to make no physical demands upon her.

So the long summer days slipped by until Gillian wrote to remind her that she expected to spend her summer holidays in Venice. It was an old promise Shelagh had made to her when she expected to be married to Camillo and her friend had taken it for granted that she would honour it. Now she informed her of the dates of her vacation and said she hoped they would be convenient.

Shelagh had not told Gillian that she had married a different man, there had been no need as Cesare had the same name and initial as his son and in her letters she always referred to him as her husband. She could not bring herself to tell of her humiliation and heartbreak. Actually they corresponded infrequently and it was easy to be impersonal. But Gillian had set her heart upon another holiday in Italy and declared she was longing to see her again. 'I hope you haven't become too grand to remember your old friends,' she concluded.

Shelagh's first reaction was to concoct an excuse to put her off, and then even as she sought to find one, discovered she was eager to revive their girlish friendship. Rita was only a child and Alice Barnes had little in common with her, Cesare was aloof, and she realised that she was lonely. Tentatively she asked her husband if Gillian might come, and to her surprise he welcomed the idea.

'It is not necessary to drop your old friends because you are married to me,' he told her. 'I shall be glad for you to have some young society.'

Somewhat reluctantly she set herself to disclose her husband's identity, expecting to revive the old pain, but as she wrote her explanation, she discovered that Camillo's image had become very faint and she could think of him without a pang. She could hardly recall his features; when she tried another face came between her and her attempts to reconstruct it, one no less handsome but stronger and sterner, the man who had married her but had never spoken of love. With her pen poised over the writing paper she became lost in thought. It still seemed incredible that Cesare was her husband; he was kind, fatherly and infinitely remote. She had no idea what he really felt about her—she rather doubted he felt anything at all. He accepted her because Camillo had left her in the lurch and he felt responsible for her. As for herself, she was grateful to him, anxious to please him, and she admired him ... what else? She sighed. If only he would be more friendly, she thought sadly, so that she could get to know him, then she might... but she broke off her conjectures at that point and finished her letter. She must pretend to Gillian that hers was a normal marriage, though she doubted if she could deceive her for long. No one could be so blind as to imagine Cesare was in love with her.

Cesare further surprised her by announcing that he would come with her to meet her friend at the airport.

'It will only be polite,' he explained, meeting her astonished gaze with a twinkle of amusement, 'as I am her host.'

'Yes, of course,' she returned quickly. She had forgotten that.

They crossed the lagoon in the motor launch with

Paolo at the controls. Cesare wore a formal light suit in honour of the guest and looked very much *il gran signore*. Shelagh felt a thrill of pride as she sat beside him. Gillian would have to admit that she had done very well for herself even if she had been jilted!

Gillian appeared through passport control wearing a thin trouser suit and sunglasses, carrying her suitcase. At a gesture from Cesare a porter materialised where none had been before and relieved her of it. Suddenly shy, Shelagh said after their initial embrace:

'Darling, I believe you've met my husband.'

It seemed so extraordinary to be able to claim him as such even after all the weeks she had spent in his house.

'In the Piazza San Marco last year,' Gillian recalled. 'A face once seen never to be forgotten, *signore*,' she simpered.

'Enchanted to renew our acquaintance,' Cesare said gallantly, and shook her hand. Shelagh was sure Gillian was disappointed that he had not kissed it, but her friend was an unmarried girl and did not rate such a salute.

During the passage of the lagoon Gillian rattled on about the events of her journey, but her eyes were full of questions. It was, she declared, marvellous to be collected by private boat instead of a grotty old bus. Arrived at the Isola, Cesare said he would meet them again at dinner and Shelagh took her friend to her room.

'Now tell me all about it,' Gillian demanded, sitting down on the bed. 'Your letter only gave me the bare facts.'

'I told you all there is to tell,' Shelagh returned. 'Camillo let me down and Cesare stepped into the breach. I . . . I couldn't face returning to England with my tail between my legs.'

'Very noble of him,' Gillian commented. 'I suppose he'd fallen madly in love with you—older men are often quite silly about young girls.'

Shelagh winced. She could not imagine Cesare being 'silly' about anyone. Then she decided to tell the truth; there was less chance of Gillian making a faux pas if she knew the real situation.

'He seemed to think the family honour required him to make amends,' she said composedly. 'There's no question of love on either side. It's a marriage of convenience for Rita's sake.'

'Ah, the little girl.'

'Yes. I get on very well with Rita. She's a dear child.'

Gillian stared at her friend's quiet face. The Italian sun had turned her skin to a fine golden shade which made her hair look lighter and her eyes greener, but in spite of her glowing colour she had an aloof, virginal appearance, very different from that of a loving bride. She said bluntly: 'You mean you don't sleep with him?'

Warm colour ran up under Shelagh's thin skin and she turned her face away. 'That wasn't in the bargain.'

'Why ever not?' Gillian demanded. 'He's still a virile man, any woman can see that, and you're an attractive girl. Does he think you're too young or some such rubbish?'

'I don't know, I haven't asked him,' Shelagh replied flippantly. 'Anyway, I don't want ... that. I ... I loved Camillo.' Unconsciously she used the past tense.

'But you're over that,' Gillian insisted.

Shelagh discovered with surprise that she was. Mention of his name no longer caused her a pang. Camillo had become a mere shadow.

'I believe I am,' she exclaimed.

'But perhaps your chivalrous husband,' Gillian's tone was sarcastic, 'is unaware that you're cured?'

Shelagh shrugged her shoulders. 'He's not interested.'

'But he ought to be. Why don't you try to make him interested?'

Shelagh walked to the window and gazed out at the smooth lawns bordered by the tall spikes of cypresses. All three rooms, hers, Cesare's and the guest room, were in front of the house above the portico. The ground floor bedroom that she had first seen was, she subsequently discovered, used by Camillo upon his infrequent visits. For that reason she avoided it. Much time and energy was spent upon keeping the grass green with repeated waterings. Everything inside and outside the house spoke of affluence. Cesare's various enterprises must be profitable, yet he had not given her an allowance, nor seemed to notice that her scanty wardrobe composed of the things she had brought with her needed replenishing; even her small and few expenses she paid for out of her own savings. She existed like a guest in Cesare's house and he was definitely not interested in clothing her. Though he had talked of dressing her properly he had done nothing about it. She would have to approach him soon about a winter outfit, and the thought was repugnant to her.

'I prefer his indifference,' she said.

'Don't be a fool,' Gillian admonished her. 'He isn't mean, is he?'

'He's most generous.'

'You surprise me. That dress you're wearing is one you brought out from England. Don't you deserve something better? Or are you regarded only as a sort of unpaid nursemaid to his child? May I ask what you've got out of this so-called marriage?'

Shelagh swung round her eyes blazing.

'He saved my face and gave me his name, together

with a refuge. What more could I expect?'

'Plenty more if I were you. Don't you realise you've no security at all? If you haven't the sense to make him do his duty, he can annul the marriage any time he chooses if it's not been consummated. I wouldn't like to live with that hanging over my head.'

'Oh, Cesare would never do that,' Shelagh declared, but the chill of doubt settled on her mind. Was that why he was always so aloof? He wanted to leave the way clear for a dissolution of the marriage if she did not come up to his expectations. He had made a gesture to repair the injury Camillo had done to her, but he meant to make sure to keep a way out. He had said Rita needed a mother, but when she went to boarding school that need would lessen. True, he had mentioned making provision for her, and that he would do, though he had overlooked her present requirements; if he wished to be rid of her she would be pensioned off. Sudden panic filled her, as she suddenly realised how much she had come to rely upon him. She could not bear to be banished from his presence.

'If you've any sense,' Gillian was saying forcibly, 'you'll do your best to ... er ... consolidate your position. Forget Camillo, he's a rat anyway, and make Cesare your lover. You always were a good-looker, Shee, and now you're quite beautiful, so you shouldn't find it difficult once you've broken through your inhibitions. He's no fish, that's obvious.' She paused and looked at Shelagh penetratingly. 'Has he any other attachments?'

That was something Shelagh had already questioned, but she was not going to betray her suspicions to her friend.

'None that I know of,' she said lightly. 'Should he have?'

'He doesn't look like a monk,' Gillian returned. 'And he's Italian.'

Cherishing her grief and nursing her supposedly broken heart, Shelagh had until that moment viewed Cesare's possible erotic adventures with detachment, but now she knew that she was healed, her complacency began to crumble. She believed Cesare was an honourable man, but did he consider he owed fidelity to a woman who was only a wife in name?

But she had had enough of Gillian's probing which she had invited by her rash disclosures and she said conventionally:

'Thank you for your advice, I'll consider it. Now would you like a bath or a shower after your journey? Then we'll have a cup of tea on the terrace. I always make it myself, not trusting our Italian cook, who makes it by pouring warm water on to tea-bags!'

Gillian opted for a shower and Shelagh left her with her heart full of misgivings, which she tried in vain to stifle. Her old love was dead, but the last thing she wanted was to become involved in a new one. Yet Cesare had become an important factor in her life and she would hate to be parted from him. Would he in time come to find, as Gillian suggested, their present arrangement unsatisfactory? She felt uneasy and insecure.

Gillian's advent seemed to stir Cesare to some sense of his shortcomings along the lines their guest had suggested. When Shelagh came into the *salotto* before dinner wearing the green silk dress she had already worn so many times, he greeted her with a slight frown. They were alone as they were early.

'You seem to be short of gowns, *cara*, and I have been remiss,' he told her. 'I intended to wait until we go to Genova and have you fitted out there by one of our best couture houses, since we do not entertain here. You must go into Venezia tomorrow and buy yourself some dazzling creation to impress your English friend. I will arrange it in the morning. I would not have her believe I am niggardly.'

Shelagh flushed at this unexpected sequel to her own thinking.

'It isn't really necessary. I don't need many clothes here.'

'I say it is,' he returned arrogantly. 'But there is something I can do now to remedy my thoughtlessness. Come with me.'

She followed him into the room he used for business where there was a small wall safe. Unlocking it, he took out a flat case.

'I meant to give this to you before,' he told her, opening it, 'but there has been no occasion to wear it. You shall tonight.'

The case contained a necklace of emeralds set in gold filigree, a costly and beautiful thing of glittering green fire. He lifted it out.

'Turn round.'

'But, Cesare...' she began to protest.

'Turn round.' It was an imperious command. Shelagh obeyed, and felt the metal cold upon her neck as he placed the necklace upon it, and his fingers on her nape as he fastened the clasp. Her sensitive skin registered his touch, sending a quiver along her nerves. His hands dropped to her shoulders as he pushed her gently towards a mirror hanging on the wall. Her eyes took the colour of the stones, and the ornament enhanced her whole appearance, but she was more conscious of his face, dark and intent, reflected over her shoulders with a certain avidness in his eyes that she had never seen before.

'It's too valuable, Cesare,' she objected. 'And you shouldn't give me jewels.'

'*Mamma mia,* who should I give them to but to you? This is an old-fashioned family piece that has not seen the light of day since Carlotta died. It is time it was on show again.'

Shelagh was about to say she did not want gems because she was not in reality his wife as Carlotta had been, but she heard Gillian calling her from the other room and it flashed into her mind that the necklace would indicate to her that she was something more than Rita's nursemaid. Her scruples vanished as she murmured:

'It's lovely, I don't know how to thank you.'

'Perhaps one day I will show you how,' he returned cryptically. 'But our guest awaits us.'

He dropped his hands from her shoulders and ceremoniously took her arm to lead her back into the *salotto.* His face was an urbane blank and she decided the strange expression she had seen over her shoulder in the mirror must have been a distortion of the glass.

Rita and her governess joined them. Cesare insisted that his daughter should be properly dressed for the meal and she exchanged with reluctance the shorts and shirt she wore all day for a frock.

Giovanna had always had charge of Rita's wardrobe and she jealously refused to let Miss Barnes interfere. The latter would have shown better taste, and Rita in the frills and furbelows of the housekeeper's choice resembled a little doll.

Looking round the dinner table, Shelagh thought they were an uninteresting trio to entertain the lively Gillian, who devoted her attention to Cesare as he was the only male present. Her audacious sallies made him laugh, bringing a vivacity to his rather austere features that made him look much younger. Shelagh felt conscience-stricken. Wrapped in her sorrows, she had made no effort to entertain him herself. Their rather boring dinner chat usually centred round Margarita and her doings, so it was not surprising that he frequently sought more amusing company. Rita resented the shift of focus and in a pause while Gillian was helping herself to the fruit and cream the maid was offering to her, the child said loudly:

'You do not ask what I have been doing all day, Papa *mio*.'

Her father turned to her with an indulgent smile.

'Has it been much different from other days, *piccolina*? You do your lessons and take your siesta...'

She interrupted. '*Sí*, and while you go in the boat to meet the *signorina inglesa*, I must sleep. It is not fair!'

Miss Barnes interposed hastily, 'Rita, you're being very rude to your father. Little girls can't expect to be taken everywhere with grown-up people.'

'I do,' Rita announced pugnaciously. 'I want to go to all places with Papa and Mamma.' She glanced at Shelagh. 'You don't love me any more now the *inglesa* has come, but I don't care. I don't like you.'

It was the first time she had called Shelagh Mamma. Usually she used her name. Shelagh had been diffident about assuming a maternal appellation with this child who actually was nearer her age than her father was. The 'Mamma' was, she was aware, an attempt to assert Rita's claim to her, since the child feared she would be excluded now Shelagh had a friend of her own age. It would have been more diplomatic to have included the little girl in the reception committee, but Cesare had thought she would interfere with the friends' reunion, which was exactly how Rita had interpreted her exclusion. Usually a well-mannered child, jealousy was making her aggressive, and her grey eyes were vindictive as she glared at her stepmother.

'Margarita, *basta*! You are not to speak to Shelagh

like that,' Cesare told her sternly. 'Apologise at once or leave the room.'

He only gave her her full name when he was annoyed with her.

Rita thrust out her underlip, jumped up from her chair and stalked out of the dining room. Cesare raised his brows as he watched her.

'If she behaves so badly, she must go to school in the autumn,' he decreed.

'She was feeling neglected because I left her alone all day,' Shelagh defended her.

'You must not let her monopolise you,' Cesare declared. 'You spoil her. She must learn you have other commitments.'

All very well when you leave us so much alone together, Shelagh thought, but she said nothing. Miss Barnes saw an opportunity to put forward her own views.

'Isn't it a mistake to allow her to sit up for dinner?' she asked tentatively. 'Biscuits and milk before she goes to bed would be much more suitable.'

'We have been into that before,' Cesare reminded her. 'She is Italian, remember, and Italian *ragazzini* dine with their parents.' He turned to Gillian with a charming smile. 'Please to forgive this little domestic crisis. Rita is normally a good little girl. It is not often that she is rude. Do not allow her behaviour to embarrass you.'

Gillian disclaimed all embarrassment.

'Step relationships are difficult for children,' she said airily. 'It takes time to adjust to them, so we must make allowances.'

Shelagh could have kicked her. She and Rita had had no difficulty in adjusting to each other until she had come.

Gillian looked archly at her host and went on, 'I

hope Shee doesn't neglect you for your daughter. Some women's maternal instincts are so much stronger than their other emotions.'

Cat, thought Shelagh, and Cesare gave his guest a quizzical glance.

'I assure you my wife is never neglectful,' he returned, and turned his gaze on Shelagh with a questioning look.

Shelagh began to wish she had not been quite so frank in her confidences to Gillian. If anyone was to be accused of neglect in their relationship, it was her husband, but she wanted no intimacies with any man after Camillo's betrayal, surely she had made that plain to Gillian? Her friend's brown eyes were sparkling with malice, and glancing at Cesare so suave and elegant at the head of his table, she knew she was being condemned as an utter idiot. Hitherto Cesare's attitude towards her had been almost paternal, but recalling his face in the glass behind her and his hands on her shoulders, she became confused. Supposing he decided to demand his marital dues? Would she be shocked, appalled or revolted? She did not know, but it would definitely be exciting.

Cesare broke off his careless banter with Gillian to say to her:

'You are very quiet, *mia cara*. Not brooding over Rita's rebellion, are you?'

With a start she realised that she had completely forgotten the child.

'Of course not, but I'll go and say goodnight to her, with your permission. I don't like to think of her being unhappy.'

'You will insist upon an apology.'

'I don't think that will be necessary.' As he seemed about to protest, she added: 'Please allow me to manage Rita in my own way.'

Their eyes met. In his was a glint of anger, hers defiance. For a moment she thought he was going to forbid her to go to the child, but he shrugged his shoulders and turned to Gillian.

'While my wife is occupied with my naughty daughter, shall we take coffee on the terrace, Signorina Dawson?'

'Please, *signore,*' Gillian protested, 'must we be so formal? My name is Gillian, or as Cam called me, Giulia.'

Cesare frowned at the mention of his son.

'I had forgotten that you met that reprobate.' Then he smiled. 'I cannot be less friendly than he was. *Avanti,* Giulia.'

Shelagh went upstairs to Rita's room after witnessing Cesare and Gillian's exit arm in arm. He was being very gallant to her friend, but she could not believe that he was really attracted to her—or could he be? Perhaps he enjoyed her pertness, and of course she was a change. Shelagh had never before considered his taste with regard to women, and certainly his manner towards the newcomer was *not* paternal.

Rita's room was at the back of the house connected to that of her governess by a small sitting room where she did her lessons. On a shelf along one wall was a collection of dolls in the national costumes of countries all over the globe. Shelagh had been shown them with pride. She recognised the Irish colleen by her red cloak, the Welsh girl by her tall hat and the Scottish lassie by her tartan, but England she had failed to identify. The dominant partner in the quartet had no distinctive costume.

Rita was, as Shelagh had expected, crying, her hair in a tangled disorder on her pillow, her face swollen with tears. Miss Barnes had undressed her, been angrily dismissed and had left her to her woe.

They effected a watery reconciliation, Shelagh assuring the child that Gillian's arrival did not mean that she would be left out, except when she had other duties she must perform.

'I have to go to Venezia tomorrow morning,' she told her. 'But you'll have your lessons to do. In the afternoon we'll all swim.'

'Does that one ... your *inglesa* ... swim?'

'Yes, but not as well as you do. I'll bring you a present from the city. What would you like?'

Rita considered. 'A little donkey with panniers filled with bonbons,' she decided. 'And you do love me best?'

'I do, darling, you're my own girl.'

Only she was not. Vaguely Shelagh wondered if she would ever have a child of her own and if so how Rita would react to it. But if she did it would be Cesare's, and probably he did not want any more children, with Camillo a disappointment and Rita a problem.

'You have a funny smile—what you thinking about?' Rita demanded.

'Unlikely happenings,' Shelagh told her. 'Or as you might say, fairy tales. *Buona notte, mia bambina.*' She kissed the child goodnight.

The garden was bathed in moonlight when Shelagh stepped out on to the terrace that overlooked it. The cypresses were dark sentinels among the delicate foliage of mimosa and tamarisk, and the night was scented by the various perfumes from the flowers planted among white ghostly statues. A night for romance, for tender whisperings and close embraces in the sweet-smelling shadows. But I've done with romance, Shelagh thought sourly, it's a snare and delusion.

Cesare and Gillian were imbibing coffee in cosy intimacy, and Shelagh felt almost an intruder as she sat down beside them. Gillian was manipulating the coffee percolator and poured her out a cup without interrupting her chatter.

'And so you see, London is rightly called the swinging capital,' she concluded. 'I bet even Rome can't equal it.'

'Giulia has been describing to me the life in modern London,' Cesare said lazily, 'and the permissive society. I must say I am not impressed. I find it decadent.'

'Like the last days of the Roman Empire?' Shelagh suggested.

'Precisely, the final stages of all great civilisations.'

'Oh, you're stuffy!' Gillian cried. 'What's wrong with fun and games?'

'The early Christians might have told you when they faced the lions to make a Roman holiday.'

'Ah, your ancestors.' Gillian's eyes gleamed. 'Are you cruel, Cesare?'

'I trust not, but most men have a streak of cruelty in them.'

'Not you,' Shelagh said firmly.

He turned his head towards her. 'You know me so well.'

He did not make it a question, but it was one she asked herself. How well did she know him? Only his surface appearance.

Gillian said: 'I think it adds to a man's fascination.'

'You would like a husband who beat you? I believe some women do. But I am not so primitive. *Ecco*, I see your visit will not be a success unless we can find a cavalier for you.'

'I'm quite content with you,' Gillian purred, touching his sleeve.

'Ah, but I have my occupations.' He moved his arm surreptitiously out of reach of her predatory fingers. 'Besides, I grow old.'

'Rubbish, mature men are much more attractive

than boys,' she declared vehemently.

'But only boys can play at love lightheartedly, and I am the ... what do you say ... paterfamilias with a wife and child.'

A wife who is no wife, Shelagh could almost hear the indiscreet words, but Gillian did not utter them. Cesare's profile was ivory in the moonlight, the high-bridged nose and chiselled features proclaiming his aristocratic lineage. Shelagh was not surprised that Gillian found him attractive, and she was glad that he had checked her advances, or was that only because she was present? What had they discussed while she had been absent, London, or other subjects? She hoped not herself. Gillian with her restless search for sexual pleasure was not to be trusted, but surely she would draw the line at attempting to seduce her best friend's husband? Unfortunately she knew he did not sleep with his wife and that might cause her to consider he was fair game. She had been a fool to confide in her.

Cesare inquired about his daughter and smiled satirically when Shelagh told him they had made it up.

'She was very sorry,' she said, omitting to mention Rita had not made the formal apology he had requested.

They made some further desultory conversation, and then he suggested that it was bedtime as they were going shopping in the morning, which would be tiring in the heat unless they made an early start. He had given Paolo orders to take them across immediately after breakfast.

'Won't you be coming with us?' Gillian asked plaintively.

'I shall be gone before you are up.'

'Doesn't she get up to see you off?'

'No. I am a bear with a sore head in the early morning. She has *prima colazzione* in her room, as yours will be brought to you also.' He stood up. 'Shall we say goodnight?'

Reluctantly Gillian rose to her feet. It was a definite dismissal and even she dared not protest, and she had no wish to stay out on the terrace when he had gone.

'I thought Italians stayed up for most of the night,' she grumbled as Shelagh went with her to her room.

'Well, it is after midnight,' Shelagh pointed out. 'And he does have to make an early start.' She gave Gillian a mischievous glance. 'As we get older we do need some sleep.'

'You talk as if you were Darby and Joan,' Gillian gibed. 'And you're far from being that . . . in any sense.'

Shelagh made no rejoinder to this barb. Arrived at Gillian's bedroom, she switched on the light, which caught the jewels about her neck with points of fire.

'That's a gorgeous necklace,' Gillian remarked, eyeing it acquisitively. 'So he's not so indifferent as you made out. You're lucky, Shee, he's a dream and I'd give a lot to be in your shoes. Aren't you glad Cam walked out on you?'

Shelagh made some non-committal reply to this tactless question. She was not ready to admit that . . . not yet.

CHAPTER SIX

SHELAGH went to her own room and took off the glittering bauble from her neck, letting it fall in a heap of green fire upon her dressing table. She changed her dress for a filmy negligée, one she had bought for her wedding night, and was brushing her hair when someone knocked upon her door.

She opened it expecting to see Gillian, but it was Cesare who stood upon the threshold. He never came to her room and for a split second apprehension showed in her eyes as she wondered why he had come. That he noticed it was clear from the ironic gleam which came into his.

'Do not be alarmed, *mia bella,*' he told her. 'I had forgotten that you need money for your expedition tomorrow.' He held out to her a bundle of lire notes and a card. 'I have an account at that establishment, and anything that you buy there can be credited to me. They have some passable garments.'

She thanked him with heightened colour, feeling oddly shamed, which was uncalled-for. She was his legal wife and he wanted her to dress to fit that position; but she gave so little in return for his generosity.

'I ... I'm deeply indebted to you already,' she faltered. 'The more you give me the guiltier I feel.'

He leaned against the door jamb regarding her appreciatively. The artificial light shone upon her hair, burnishing its red-gold, and the slight curves of her body were visible through the thin material of her negligée.

'Guilty? *Dio mio,* why should you feel guilt? You are fulfilling our bargain admirably.'

Shelagh crossed her arms over her bosom and drooped her head, letting her loosened hair veil her face.

'I feel I should give ... more.'

He straightened himself and his mouth set in a grim line.

'Yet when you saw me at your door you looked frightened. I take no unwilling women, and I abhor sacrifices.'

She dropped her arms and raised her head.

'You find plenty who are willing?' she asked.

'The world being what it is, I do, including one you have introduced yourself.'

Shelagh drew a deep breath. 'Gillian doesn't mean ...'

'I know very well what she means,' he interrupted, his voice very cold and stern. 'But you gave her encouragement, did you not? Even she would not make advances if she believed you were a loving wife.'

Shelagh started guiltily. Could Gillian have betrayed her confidences? She must have done, for he went on icily: 'I would prefer if in future you kept the circumstances of our marriage to yourself, it would be less embarrassing for me. She had the presumption to take me to task about my ... er ... neglect.'

Colour stained Shelagh's face and she could not meet his eyes.

'I always tell Gill everything,' she said defensively.

'Then your discretion is at fault.'

'It's all very well, but I haven't any people of my own,' she cried a little wildly. 'She's like a sister, and women need to talk.'

'An unfortunate failing.' He was being sarcastic. 'And one that has done infinite harm in all societies. I must ask you to restrain the urge in future.'

She started at him reproachfully. 'You're not human!'

He moved restlessly and a glitter came into his cold grey eyes.

'We had better say goodnight before you discover I am only too human.'

It was on the tip of Shelagh's tongue to say that she wanted him to show his humanity, but his cool aloofness chilled her. He had been reprimanding her severely for a very trivial fault and she resented it. Then a little imp of mischief entered her. He had seemed amused by Gillian's method's, though now he was pretending to disapprove of them. Well, she also could be provocative. Glancing at him slyly, she said demurely:

'Aren't you going to kiss me goodnight?'

He started as if he had received an electric shock and his eyes slid over her sensuously, noting every detail of her becoming apparel, her loose hair and exquisite moulding of neck and shoulders. Fire kindled in his eyes and he took a step towards her. Involuntarily she recoiled. Cesare stopped and passed his hand across his forehead.

'No,' he said hoarsely. 'Do not tempt me. It would not stop at kissing.'

Abruptly he turned round and strode away down the passage away from her.

Shelagh closed her door, unsure whether she was relieved or disappointed. Familiar emotions were stirring within her. She had been determined not to fall in love again, she had suffered too much through Camillo, but she was very much afraid she was about to do so. If she did, what then? Cesare did not love her; he had married her for varying reasons, but he had never suggested love was one of them. He might come to desire her, she had recognised the look in his eyes, but it was only a transitory emotion. Tomorrow he would have forgotten it amid his many interests and possibly other women. Gillian's teasing and her own invitation had aroused him, for as her friend said, he was still a virile man, and he had been tempted to assuage his passion upon her ... as was his right, but he had not done so, because he had seen her apprehension ... distaste ... however he had interpreted her shrinking. Why had she been so afraid?

Her reactions were complex, she was ashamed that her love for Camillo had faded so quickly. It was only about eight months since she had last seen him, but during that Christmas visit, she recalled that she had been repelled by his importunities. Dimly she had begun to realise that he was not the man she had thought him to be. As Cesare had told her, she had been in love with her own image of him, a very different being from the real Camillo. She could not afford to make the same mistake twice, and if the ultimate happened, she might find herself at the mercy of a tyrant, for she sensed there lurked a ruthlessness beneath Cesare's courteous exterior. Both his former wives had died early and he did not seem to mourn for them. She had come to distrust her judgment and still more her feelings. Not that she had been capable of such reasoning when Cesare had been with her, but instinct combined with a virginal recoil from the unknown had caused her to show fright and it had been enough to drive him from her.

The fateful moment had passed and their relationship would remain unchanged. Tomorrow everything would be as it had been before, but as Shelagh slowly discarded her wrap and lay down on her bed, she was vaguely regretful that she was lying there alone.

She woke early, recalling that she was committed to

a morning's shopping with Gillian in Venice, while Cesare was absent. Looking at her watch, she saw it was just after sunrise and he would not have left. He would be eating a lonely breakfast in the *sala di pranzo*. She had a sudden impulse to go down and join him, as surely a good wife should, instead of waiting for her coffee and rolls to be brought up to her at a later hour. She lay for a while playing with the idea and then reluctantly abandoned it. Cesare had said that he was irritable in the early morning, 'a bear with a sore head', and would not welcome her appearance. He had ordered their daily routine to suit their joint convenience and would see no reason to alter it. She had obeyed his wishes unquestioningly because she had been wholly indifferent to how she lived, absorbed in her heartbreak. But Gillian's coming had jolted her out of her apathy. This custom of breakfasting alone was unsociable. Rita, poor child, was left to Miss Barnes's ministrations and it would be more like a family if they all ate together. It was possible that Cesare felt his daughter and the dim governess were more than he could face first thing in the morning before a day's work, but there was no reason why she should not join them. During these hot summer days it would be pleasant to have the meal out on the terrace. She would ask Giovanna to arrange it. It was only a very trivial matter, but it marked a significant change in Shelagh's attitude, a first step towards taking an active interest in the running of her home.

In due course Paolo announced that he was at their disposal and landed them at the Molo. The Marzaria, which started at the Piazza San Marco and stretched to the Rialto, was full of excellent and expensive shops. Shelagh was at a loss where to begin. An evening dress, she supposed, and some day dresses to supplement those she already had. It was too early to consider her autumn wardrobe—besides, had not Cesare mentioned shopping in Genoa? Instead of shrinking from the prospect of the move to that city, she began to look forward to it.

The evening dress she chose was grey silk with half sleeves and a modest neckline. It was severely cut without trimmings.

'Too old,' Gillian objected. 'Do you want to look like a dowager?'

'Yes,' Shelagh returned. 'I've a position to maintain nowadays. I don't want to look like a teenager.'

'The gown has style and dignity,' the saleswoman interpolated in Italian. Shelagh, who now had a working knowledge of the language, declared that it was just what she wanted, but Cesare's reception of her purchase when she put it on that evening coincided with her friend's.

'Charming, *mia cara,* but though grey suits your colouring, it is a shade only older women and widows wear.'

'But I am older, much older,' she told him. 'Camillo killed my youth.'

His son's name was rarely mentioned between them and he frowned.

'You pay him too great a compliment,' he said coldly. He searched her face intently. 'Do you still grieve for him?'

Two days ago Shelagh would have stoutly maintained that she did. Love like hers, even for a worthless object, took a long time to die. But now she knew that she no longer cared, her sorrow had dispersed like mist before the sun, and the sun that had performed this miracle was the man standing beside her. But she could not admit that while he was still indifferent, for she discounted his flash of passion the night before. Any woman in similar circumstances could have evoked that, and she was still a little ashamed of her change of heart.

'I suppose he's not worth grieving for,' she observed evasively, and a flash of disappointment crossed Cesare's face. 'I want to become a good housewife,' she went on, 'and the servants won't take me seriously if my clothes are too frivolous.'

'No, naturally not,' he agreed with mock seriousness. 'I suggest you wear a cap on your head and a bunch of keys at your waist.'

'Now you're laughing at me,' she complained. 'I meant it, Cesare.'

'Little one, you will have plenty to learn when we go to Genoa, but I do not wish you to be weighed down by responsibilities. There will be playtime as well.'

'That's nice to know,' she returned, stifling a throb of anxiety. Then Gillian burst in upon them in a swirl of multi-coloured drapery, and Miss Barnes in brown shepherding Rita appeared from the terrace. Conversation became general.

Not only had Gillian's arrival dispelled Shelagh's apathy, but her friend's flirtatious manner towards Cesare had shocked her into a new appreciation of her husband as a man. However, he soon grew tired of Gillian's kittenish ways and dug up some young people from among his Venetian friends to come and amuse her. They played tennis, swam and went on expeditions as they had done during the previous summer, but Shelagh could no longer participate wholeheartedly, and as Cesare rarely joined them, she was the odd one out. The young men who made up the party were quite ready to flirt with her, but she did not encourage them, feeling it was beneath her dignity and an affront to her husband, nor had she any wish to do so; their advances seemed to her shallow and empty. Italian society loved to gossip, and as Cesare trusted her she had no intention of setting tongues wagging by indiscreet behaviour. Among the visitors who daily thronged the Casa was Alonso, whose surname she discovered was Pirelli. This was not surprising as he belonged to the same circle as the Barsinis and had been an acquaintance of Camillo's. The sight of him gave Shelagh a jolt, but her discomfort soon passed. Last summer seemed an aeon ago. He remembered her perfectly.

'You gave us all a surprise,' he said to her, when he was able to draw her aside. 'We thought you Camillo's bride and lo and behold, it is *il signore* himself! May I present my felicitations. He is the better man.'

A short while back these words would have stabbed her, but now she was able to laugh and return: 'I soon discovered that.'

'*Dio mio*, but you are ... what do you say ... a black horse.'

'Dark horse,' she corrected automatically, and Gillian came up to demand what they were muttering about..

'Signor Pirelli was congratulating me,' Shelagh said demurely. 'I haven't seen him since my wedding.'

'And not then.' Alonso looked aggrieved. 'So few people invited ... almost as if he was ashamed of his choice. Perhaps you do the choosing?' He leered at her.

'Of course she didn't, Cesare fell for her hook, line and sinker,' Gillian cried loyally. Whatever she said and thought privately, she would permit no slur upon Shelagh from an outsider.

'We didn't want a lot of people,' Shelagh said sweetly, wincing immediately at Gillian's inaccuracy. 'Only intimates,' which she knew the Pirellis were not.

Alonso shrugged his shoulders and went off with Gillian to the swimming pool. Naturally there had been conjectures among the Venetians about Cesare's marriage, but no one knew the truth. It was supposed that she had jilted Camillo in favour of his father, and he had gone off in despair—an explanation that though it did not present her in a favourable light, salved Shelagh's pride, nor did she mind that the local V.I.P.s had not called upon her. Time enough to make her social debut when she went to Genoa.

Three days before the end of Gillian's holiday, Cesare told them he would have to go away. They were at dinner and he apologised to the guest as he made his explanation.

'An old friend of mine has died and I must go to the funeral and stay to give his widow my help. He was crippled in an accident, since when I have managed his affairs for him; we knew he could not live very long. But you have many young friends coming to amuse you, so you will not miss me, *sí*?'

'Of course I'll miss you.' Gillian made play with her false eyelashes. 'But I'll try to console myself.' Her brown eyes narrowed. 'The widow is an old lady?'

'No, she was much younger than Tommaso, a woman in her prime.'

Something clicked in Shelagh's brain. He had never mentioned these friends of his before, not that he ever did talk about his acquaintances to her, but if he were managing their business, it might be that he visited them upon the occasions when he was absent from home. A woman with an invalid husband, a woman in her prime! Was she the mistress whose existence she had suspected for so long? Anxiously she searched Cesare's bland face, but it revealed nothing.

'Where do they live?' she asked with assumed casualness.

'At Alassio on the Ligurian coast. Tommaso has a large house there of which I am sure his widow will wish to dispose. I have long urged that they should move into a flat in Genova. They would have found it so much more convenient. Now that he is gone, I am sure she will wish to do so.'

Much more convenient—he would have easy access to her when they went to that city in the winter. Shelagh stared at her plate, while her thoughts whirled. The death of her husband would mean that this woman—he had not mentioned her name—would be free to remarry, had known she would be free since Tommaso had not been expected to live long. Wild conjectures flitted through her mind. Had they been lovers? Would Cesare now regret his own hasty marriage, seek a way to be rid of her? Gillian's remarks about an annulment recurred to her unpleasantly. Had he had this eventuality in mind when he had so readily promised that he would never force himself upon her? He knew an unconsummated marriage would be much easier to dissolve than a real one.

Cesare excused himself from taking coffee with them on the terrace as was their nightly custom. He had preparations to make, before an early start in the morning. He glanced at Shelagh, who was wearing the necklace he had given her, which embellished the plainness of her grey dress.

'As I shall not be here to protect you, it would be best to return your necklace to the safe.'

Shelagh's fingers closed over it protectively. Except for her rings, a belated engagement one and her wedding ring, it was the only jewellery he had given her. It seemed to her to be a talisman, a link with him when other links were threatened.

'Must you?' she protested. 'I'll take great care of it.'

'I am sure you would, but I would feel easier if it is in the safe.'

'Oh very well, I'll bring it . . . later.'

When he had gone, Gillian gibed: 'Are you afraid he'll give it ... to someone else?'

'No, of course not, but it seems a shame it should be put away again,' Shelagh said quickly, but Gillian had uttered her half-formed thought.

'Why doesn't he take you with him?' Gillian went on. 'Surely that would be more correct if this widow in her prime is alone?'

'He knows I couldn't leave you,' Shelagh pointed out.

'Fortuitous, wasn't it?' Gillian was eyeing her maliciously. 'I gather you've never met these pals of his?'

Shelagh moved restlessly. Gillian was crystallising her own half-formed fears.

'Doubtless I should have been introduced to them when we move to Genoa,' she said frigidly.

'Oh, doubtless, and now you'll meet the widow if she's going to live there. I hope you get on with her.'

'That remains to be seen.' Shelagh rose to her feet. 'I'd better take the necklace to Cesare.'

She had not enjoyed her friend's visit as much as she had expected. Gillian was frankly envious of her marriage and thought Shelagh did not appreciate her good fortune or she would make greater efforts to preserve it. Her barbed remarks were made with the intention of needling her into action, and her misplaced betrayal of Shelagh's confidences had been made with the best of intentions, for Gillian believed that all men were ready to take advantage of female weaknesses. She was sure Cesare would respond if Shelagh showed she was available. But Shelagh, far more sensitive, was fearful of being repulsed by her autocratic husband, and her dawning love for him, as yet unrecognised, made her vulnerable. She would not dare to hint at her suspicions, and to seek to claim her rights seemed to her presumption. She had made a bargain with him and the emotional aspect had been excluded.

When she entered his study, or as he called it, his workroom, Cesare was turning over a mass of papers on the desk before him, presumably connected with Tommaso's estate. The night being hot, he had taken off his jacket and tie, rolling up his shirt sleeves to disclose his brown, muscular arms. Usually precise in his attire, his déshabille gave him an added attraction. Mutely Shelagh laid the necklace down in front of him. He glanced up at her, frowning. Without the glitter of the gems about her throat in her neutral tinted dress the only colour about her was her hair.

'You are a ghost in that gown,' he said abruptly. 'Get yourself something brighter. With your colouring green suits you.'

'I'm tired of green,' she objected, sitting down on the hard chair on the other side of his desk. 'Most of my outfits are green, or hadn't you noticed?'

'I notice everything about you,' he returned unexpectedly.

'Do you?' She opened her eyes very wide. 'You surprise me, but green is supposed to be unlucky.'

'Have you then been so unfortunate?'

Was there a hint of reproach in his eyes? She drew her forefinger along the edge of the desk.

'I might have been much more so if it hadn't been for you,' she admitted. 'I hope you'll never regret your quixotic action.'

'Is that still worrying you? Believe me, *cara mia*, my actions are too well considered to allow of regrets.'

But he had not known his girl-friend was so soon to become a widow, and if he had regrets he would be too proud to admit them.

'If you are tired of green,' he went on, 'what about gold or blue? There are too many spectres between us for me to relish grey.'

He must mean Camillo and now this woman, only she was not a ghost but a living entity, and a dangerous one.

'Your wishes shall be obeyed, O Maestro,' she said mockingly. 'In this as in all things.'

'All things?' He took her up with a glint in his eyes. 'That is a rash statement, *mia cara*. I might request something much more fundamental than a change of dress.'

She looked up quickly with terror in her eyes. Had she given him an opening to ask for an annulment of their marriage? He saw her fear and his face hardened.

'You should not express yourself so extravagantly,' he rebuked her. He stood up, picked up the necklace and went to the safe. 'I am sorry I have to leave you, but as I said, with so much youth and gaiety coming and going my absence will hardly be noted.'

Shelagh gazed yearningly at his broad shoulders and the back of his well shaped head on which the black hair for once was ruffled.

'They're all so empty-headed,' she sighed.

He swung round and she hastily lowered her eyelashes.

'Is living with me here making you old before your time?'

'Of course not,' she denied hotly. 'But I've lost my taste for frivolity. I'll be glad when Gillian's gone and the Professor comes back to resume my lessons. I feel I'm losing ground.' For Shelagh's studies had been suspended during her friend's visit.

Cesare regarded her with a dissatisfied expression.

'Perhaps it was a mistake to marry you.'

'Oh no, please, please don't say that!' she cried with such intensity that he raised his brows. 'It was the kindest thing any man could do, and I'll be eternally grateful.'

'You are still?'

'Always.'

'Gratitude grows thin after a while, and I am glad yours is perennial,' he told her, but his tone was sarcastic. He glanced at his desk. 'I still have much to do, and charming as your presence is, I shall have to ask you to leave me.'

'Oh, I'm sorry.' She sprang to her feet. 'You'll be leaving very early?'

'Long before you will be up, so this is goodnight and goodbye.'

Was it her fancy, or was there finality in his last word?

She cried desperately, 'But you will come back?'

'Naturally, in about four days' time. Why are you so agitated, Shelagh? I have been away before.'

But then she wasn't free ... Shelagh nearly blurted out the words, and swallowed hastily. Of course he would come back, if only to acquaint her with his plans, and what they might be she dared not contemplate.

'I suppose after Cam's defection I'm always apprehensive,' she explained. 'I expect to be let down.'

He swore. 'Damn that son of mine!' He added soothingly: 'Surely you know that I never would? As long as you need me I will be there.'

She ought to have been satisfied with that, but she was not. Italians were always so glib where women were concerned. She had trusted Camillo, who had been vociferous in his protestations of love and devotion. Yet he had walked out when he had found a wealthier woman. This man did not even profess to love her, so how could she hope to hold him if he wanted to go?

'Thank you,' she said flatly. 'Goodbye, Cesare.'

He picked up her limp hand and kissed her fingers. '*Ciao, piccolina*. Sleep well.'

Piccolina, little one—he regarded her as an older Rita. Shelagh went out of the room with hanging head and Cesare watched her go with a strange expression in his eyes.

—

Three days later Giovanna showed Shelagh the daily paper in which the funeral had been reported. Shelagh only read the Italian papers as part of her lessons, not always able to follow them, but she pored over this account, puzzling out every word. Tommaso's full name was the Conte di Monticelli, Tommaso Alberto Luigi, and his tragic accident had happened five years ago. His young wife had nursed him devotedly. She had been Beatrice Cavour, a famous Roman beauty. There were photographs in one of which Cesare was just recognisable, in black coat and top hat. On his arm was a veiled figure, the Contessa, but so heavily draped in black crêpe that no details were discernible.

'Il Maestro was a very intimate friend of the family,' Giovanna told her. 'When the Signora died they came to stay here. The Conte was an elderly gentleman, but the Contessa—*bella, molto bella.* They comfort my master in his bad time. Now he go to comfort her, though it happy release for the Signor Conte, he was half dead. Now he is whole dead, she find another husband *pronto.*'

'Possibly,' Shelagh agreed, and folded up the paper.

Gillian went home with many regretful sighs. 'I'll see you again next year?' she hinted.

Shelagh was non-committal. If all were well, yes, perhaps, but if Cesare were in the midst of annulment proceedings she would not want Gillian's comments.

Cesare returned from Alassio and outwardly they resumed their former tranquil existence, but there were undercurrents. The Contessa di Monticelli wrote often, presumably on business. Shelagh came to recognise the bulky envelopes on which the address was not typewritten but written in a fine Italian hand. The post arrived about midday and if Cesare were absent as he often was, Shelagh sorted the mail and put his letters in his room. Thus she had ample opportunity to study them. She suspected the envelopes contained personal matters beside documents connected with her estate. Why else should Beatrice direct them in her own hand?

Cesare answered her questions about the funeral without evasion. So, she had seen the report. Yes, it was very impressive, the Conte was well known and well liked, he would be greatly missed. The Contessa was bearing up as well as could be expected under her great loss. There were no children. A nephew was the next heir, but Tommaso had made ample provision for his widow. Yes, she had decided to live in Genova.

'When you will be presented to her, Shelagh, as soon as her mourning permits.'

'I'll look forward to it,' Shelagh said politely, and she would like to meet this woman whom she suspected of being a rival. Cesare never referred to her again, though the letters continued to come. He did not comment upon them and Shelagh was left to her conjectures. The Contessa became to her an unseen presence in the house, for Cesare's manner was often abstracted, particularly after he had heard from her, and Shelagh thought of her constantly. Her uncertainty undermined her serenity, and she could not concentrate upon her studies, for if her connection with Cesare were to end, there was no point in them. Changes were ahead when they went to Genoa in October. Rita was to attend a convent school during the day and Miss Barnes was looking for another situation. Giovanna was to stay at the Isola di Santa Lucia as caretaker.

'So we shall have a new staff?' Shelagh asked Cesare.

'Yes, and you will manage it, *sí*? By now you should be enough familiar with our ways to undertake the task.'

A prospect she found a little daunting. Giovanna was more reassuring. A skeleton staff was already in occupation, it was a permanency, and she would find the house ran 'like wheels that were oiled.' She would only have to order the meals and she knew the Signore's tastes.

'But when he entertains?'

'The custom is to give parties in a hotel,' Giovanna explained.

To a capable girl, and Shelagh was that, the position did not appear very formidable after all, and she wondered if she would have enough to do. She read up books about Genoa and found it had many entertainments to offer and places to explore. Cesare arranged for her to have a quarterly allowance and gave her a cheque book. The amount was generous and she did not like accepting it, but reflected that what she did not spend she could hand back if... That 'if' hung over her, spoiling her pleasurable excitement about the change of residence. For the Contessa Beatrice di Monticelli would be there, and Cesare could have more daily contact with her if he wished. Shelagh feared her reputed beauty and their long association would overcome any lingering scruples Cesare might have about dismissing herself. Even if he did not, Shelagh felt her position would soon become untenable.

CHAPTER SEVEN

SHELAGH opened the window over which the blinds had not yet been drawn and looked out over the harbour of Genoa spread beneath her, for the Barsini house was built on a spur of the foothills, and unlike Venice the town was backed by mountains. They, to her excited fancy, seemed forbidding, looming over a future full of pitfalls which she had been dragged forth to face after the peaceful interlude in retirement at the Isola.

The last light lingered in the sky above the glittering illuminations of the panorama of wharves, moles, streets and squares spread out along the dark water which reflected them. Among the shipping docked at the piers were several cruise ships dressed over all with coloured bulbs, among which might well be one from England making an autumn tour; England, which had become so remote since the sharp dividing line of her marriage had cut her off from all her old associations. During the day, Genoa was permeated by the hum of working cranes, trains, cars, buses and alighting and descending aircraft, but as night approached its activity slackened, and this evening it seemed almost tranquil. A wandering breeze stirred her hair, bringing with it a whiff of spice from some ship unloading in the harbour. If only she could go down and embark upon a boat which would carry her far away and escape the ordeal that lay ahead of her! For tonight she must act as hostess at a big dinner party, her debut among Cesare's business colleagues, and she felt sick with apprehension and fear of being inadequate.

With a sigh she closed the window and drew down the Venetian blind, turning back into her bedroom. It was furnished with a luxury of which she had never dreamed. The walls were panelled in white and palest pink, the carpet white bordered with pink roses and of pile so thick her bare feet sank into it as if it caressed them. The furniture itself was white and gold, French in design, and there were several gilt-mounted mirrors on the walls, The crowning glory of the room was the elegant Empire bed, draped with white organdie curtains suspended from a gold crown perched high above it, a wide bed, designed for an Emperor and an Empress in which she slept alone. Someone, she did not remember who, had let slip that it had been chosen by Carlotta d'Este when she had come here as a bride, and Cesare had seen no reason to change it. Carlotta must have shared it with him, and there conceived her child.

On the bed one of the Italian maids had laid out her evening dress, which was deceptively simply styled in Grecian fashion, with a high waist, a mere puff of sleeve and a draped skirt. It was white with a touch of gold embroidery at neck and hem, a gown Josephine Buonaparte might have worn, and with it she would wear the emerald necklace. That had been produced from the safe and lay ready on her dressing table, a heap of glittering green fire, and with it a matching bracelet which Cesare had given her upon their arrival at Genoa.

A room and clothes fit for a queen. Cesare had showered upon her everything that money could buy, almost as if he sought to make up to her for what he could not give her and what was worth more than all the furnishings and fripperies put together—his love.

She had learned that the Contessa was installed in Genoa, and Cesare was probably seeing her frequently. It might even be that his generosity was prompted by guilt. Didn't the best novels say that erring husbands eased their consciences with jewels? Hence the emerald bracelet, but Cesare owed her no fidelity that had not been part of the bargain.

With a little sigh, Shelagh sat down on the brocade-covered stool in front of the triple-mirrored dressing table and started to apply her simple make-up. She needed no foundation, she was still tanned by the Venetian sun, merely green eye-shadow, mascara and a soft pink lipstick. The glass reflected her slight figure, ridiculously youthful in her silk slip for the part of sophisticated matron which she had to play that night. She regarded herself critically, addressing her mirrored image in a wistful murmur.

'You aren't bad looking, and you're young, much younger than the Contessa di Monticelli, I'm sure. What has she got that I haven't? Cesare treats me like a child, but I'm growing up, fast.'

But not fast enough. She still lacked sophistication, and that the Contessa would possess in abundance.

Almost defiantly she twisted up her hair on top of her head, hoping it would make her look older. In the couture-styled dress and the jewels she would appear the perfect hostess even if she could not act the part, and perhaps for once Cesare would notice her as a woman.

The image she presented in her classical dress with her high-piled hair and gleaming jewels was reassuring. Her neck and arms gleamed with a pearly lustre and her eyes looked big and mysterious. Pleased with her appearance, she turned from the mirror as a knock came on her door.

'*Avanti!*' she called.

The door opened to reveal Cesare on the threshold, magnificent in his dress clothes, and her heart sank. He looked every inch a distinguished, elegant aristocrat, and she was presumptuous to suppose that she could ever hope to physically attract this handsome, assured man of the world who had known so many beautiful women before he had ever met her. She was foolish to imagine he could be swayed by youth and good looks alone, who had had his pick of birth, brains and beauty in his time. His first wife had been lovely to look at, but he had found her insipid. Carlotta had been a great lady, and a Countess was angling for him, while she was only a pretty little nobody he had taken under his protection to right a wrong.

Cesare advanced into the room, his eyes fixed upon her, and her confidence returned with an upsurge of triumph, for in their grey depths was an expression even her innocence could not mistake, the glow of desire.

'*Dio mio—é bellissima!*'

The soft Italian syllables were a caress and Shelagh's pulses raced. The many mirrors on the walls reflected her red-gold hair and shimmering figure, and the man's lithe elegance as he came towards her, for once shaken out of his urbane self-command.

'*Amore mia! Mia vita!*' he murmured huskily.

Shelagh's heart gave a great leap. Had she won before she had even begun to fight? She swayed towards him, anticipating that he was about to take her into his arms.

But they were interrupted.

Before Cesare had reached her a small dark tornado flew into the room, interposing itself between the man and girl, hurling itself upon Shelagh.

Rita was in her nightgown and sobbing hysterically. Shelagh knelt down and gathered the child into her arms. She had said goodnight to her before she had started to dress, and as it was earlier than usual she had explained that she was going out. Concetta, the Italian girl who had replaced Miss Barnes, would put her to bed and keep an eye upon her.

'What is it, darling?' Shelagh asked. 'Where's Concetta?'

'I hate Concetta,' Rita gulped. 'I want you, Mamma. I don't like this place, I hate that horrible convent! Take me back to Venice.'

'This is absurd.' Cesare spoke sternly. 'Shelagh, you are crumpling your dress. Rita, you must never enter Mamma's room without knocking, and you should be in bed. Go back to your room at once!'

He was very pale and his eyes were glittering. The child's sudden entrance had impinged upon a wave of emotion that had recoiled like a snapped elastic. Shelagh had less difficulty in adapting herself to the child's need.

'The poor mite seems very upset,' she defended her. 'What was it, darling? A bad dream?'

Rita seized the pretext eagerly. '*Sí, sí*, a nasty dream. I come to you, Mamma, to drive the bogies away.'

She gazed appealingly at her father from the shelter of Shelagh's encircling arms, but his face did not soften. She had chosen a bad moment to break in upon them. She had thwarted whatever impulse had driven Cesare towards his wife and her obvious belief that she could impose upon Shelagh irritated him. Giovanna in her role of foster-mother had indulged Camillo in his infancy and he had turned out very badly.

'She has no time to bother with you now,' he said frostily. 'You are making up excuses to delay her. You can't go back to Venice, and you told me you liked going to school. As for your bad dream, I don't believe you had one. Go back to your room—*presto*!'

'I won't!' Rita shrieked, her small face contorted with fury at this failure of her appeal. 'I won't, I won't! I want Mamma, my new Mamma, that you gave me to look after me. She doesn't want to go to your horrid party. Mamma, stay with me!'

Out of the mouth of babes ... Shelagh thought. Rita had gauged her attitude correctly, but Cesare was not likely to accept such an excuse.

The child's rage woke answering passion in him. Two pairs of grey eyes regarded each other defiantly, then Cesare muttered an oath and going to the door called loudly for Concetta.

'You are a naughty, ill-mannered child,' he told his daughter, turning back into the room, and Concetta came running in.

'Is this how you tend the *signorina*?' Cesare demanded icily. 'Take her back to bed at once and make sure she stays there.'

'*Scusi, scusi, signore*,' the maid apologised. 'She is cunning, that one, she gave me the slip ...'

'*Basta!*' Cesare snapped. 'Margarita, go *at once*!'

Rita's temper had given place to anguished tears. She clung desperately to Shelagh, who with difficulty detached her clinging arms.

'Go along, darling,' she murmured gently.

Concetta stepped forward to take Rita's hand, but her charge pushed it aside and still hiccuping with obviously forced sobs, interposed with tearful injections of 'Mamma!' crept out of the room with a last reproachful glance at Shelagh as she reached the door.

'It might be as well to send her to the convent as a boarder,' Cesare observed.

'Oh no,' Shelagh protested. 'She's much too young.'

'Then you must be more strict with her.' He looked at his watch. 'Get your wrap, my dear, or we shall be late.'

Shelagh glanced into the mirror hoping that Rita had not mussed her hair, and saw Cesare was watching her with an enigmatical expression. Surely he could not be jealous of his own daughter? Gillian had suggested he could be, but the idea was absurd. She moved to the wardrobe and extricated the simulated silver fox fur Cesare had given her. She had refused to accept the genuine article, declaring it was wicked to kill such a beautiful animal for her adornment, and Cesare had acceded to her request with indulgent amusement. He took the fur from her and placed it gently around her, his hands lingering on her shoulders. The intimacy of the action and his presence in her room was affecting her strongly. He bent his head and kissed the nape of her neck.

The touch of his lips shot like fire through her veins, but she was too upset by his harshness to his daughter to soften towards him.

'*Molto bella,*' he murmured, and she realised it was only a piece of Italian gallantry, towards a good-looking woman. It meant nothing. She pulled the fur closer about her shoulders and moved away from him.

'I'll just look in at Rita and say goodnight,' she told him.

'You will please to do no such thing,' Cesare forbade her. 'The whole episode was manufactured to delay you, and she was abominably rude. I detest rudeness, especially in females.'

Shelagh was reminded of Rita's behaviour when Gillian had come to stay, which had incensed him, but that interlude had ended in reconciliation and a goodnight kiss. She would feel better if she saw Rita before she left.

She said appealingly, 'Mayn't I kiss her goodnight?'

'I presume you've already done that once.' Cesare

took hold of her arm. 'I cannot condone scenes like the one she made tonight.'

'Aren't you being a little unkind? She'd had a bad dream and came to m ... us for comfort.'

'The bad dream was your idea, not hers. I forbid you to go to Margarita.'

'Forbid!' Shelagh's green eyes flashed, and a surge of revolt surged through her. 'I insist upon seeing her before we go.'

The grip on her arm tightened and Cesare's voice became icy.

'Shelagh, you are my wife, not Rita's nursemaid. Both of you owe me obedience. Rita is a wilful child. All she wanted was to draw attention to herself because we were going out. I will not have my daughter spoilt by misplaced indulgence.'

The fire faded from Shelagh's eyes and she drooped her head, a faint blush of humiliation staining her now pale face. She was Cesare's wife, he had a right to claim her obedience and Rita was his child, not hers, and it was for him to say how she should be raised.

Realising her rebellion was subdued, Cesare withdrew his hand from her arm and indicated the door.

'Come, or we shall be unpardonably late.'

Shelagh passed through into the corridor and down the handsome marble staircase, feeling almost physically ill after the welter of emotions through which she had passed. Being highly strung, her nerves reacted upon her body in the form of a migraine type headache. She felt one developing now. She suspected Cesare so resented Rita's appearance because she had interrupted ... what? She had been conscious that his sensual feelings had been aroused by her appearance, but she did not attempt to deceive herself that it had been more than a momentary desire. It had died when Rita had burst in upon them, but it was unfair to take his frustration out upon the child. Hadn't he told her that part reason for their marriage was to give Rita the mother she needed? Yet when she tried to act like one he said she spoilt her. How dared he forbid her—rage shook her—forbid her to say goodnight to the child! She hated him and she would not play hostess at this party of his; he could not force her to do so.

As they reached the front door, she turned to make her decision known, but he forestalled her, saying:

'I seem to recall that last time we had a disagreement about Rita you told me my wishes should be obeyed in all things.'

'But that was in Venice,' she began, 'before...' Before she had known about Beatrice di Monticelli, when she had felt secure.

'Does locality affect your loyalty?' he asked with a quizzical smile.

'No, of course not.' She squared her shoulders, her resolution fading. She could not draw back now, he would despise her utterly for such weakness, even though she had got a genuine headache.

He gestured that she should proceed through the door the servant had opened for her. Such ostentation, she thought drearily, when they were quite capable of opening the door for themselves. She went through with her tawny head held high, and Cesare passed her on the steps that led down into the street to be ready to help her into the front seat of the car parked below them. She shivered at the touch of his hand and his lip curled.

'Hating me for my paternal severity?' he asked ironically.

'Loathing you,' she returned vehemently.

He laughed, not taking her seriously, and slid in beside her. He preferred to drive himself when the chaffeur could be dispensed with.

Shelagh sank into the luxurious upholstery of the Mercedes, the ache in her head becoming like a steel band across her forehead. She was tense as a drawn bow, convinced the evening was foredoomed before it began.

At the hotel, there was much bowing and scraping by an army of waiters and ushers as they were escorted into the lounge where Cesare was to receive his guests. They were mainly middle-aged people, stout business men with their opulent wives, for the most part fighting a losing battle against advancing years and avoirdupois. Shelagh stood like a white ghost with a fixed smile on her face while they were presented to her, the men kissing her hand, the women her cheek, and not one of their names could she afterwards recall. She tried to make polite rejoinders to their fulsome compliments, for after all this was her first appearance as Cesare Barsini's girl bride, but what with nerves and her migraine her Italian deserted her and she was reduced to stammering English.

The meal was a nightmare; every morsel she tried to eat made her feeling of nausea worse and the wine made her head reel. She tried to converse with the men on either side of her, but one had no English and the other found her nervous remarks boring. At the end of the meal they all toasted her, and she was so confused she did not know whether to stand up or remain seated, and she caught Cesare's sardonic smile. Was he thinking he was hardly to be congratulated upon acquiring such a gauche and stupid bride? He covered up for her, answering the well-wishers with a flowery speech in which he referred to himself as a lucky man to have won so much beauty and grace, but the glance he bestowed upon her was not lover-like. Worse was to follow, for she did not notice when Cesare signalled to her to conduct the ladies to the lounge, until a large, ugly woman indicated her omission. She rose hurriedly and knocked over her untouched wine, instinctively dabbing at the mess with her table napkin instead of leaving it for the waiter to deal with.

'*Permesso, signora,*' the man said, and aware of Cesare's frown at her clumsiness, she hastily fled to the lounge. It seemed to her the other women were throwing amused glances in her direction and she was sure they were laughing at her gaucherie. At least she was thankful she did not have to pour the coffee, which the waiters served. She longed for Cesare to come to her and restore her confidence, but he was engrossed in conversation with his colleagues. As usually happens in continental gatherings, the men all foregathered at one end of the room, the women at the other. Feeling sure she could not join in the domestic tittle-tattle of the older ladies, Shelagh retreated with her coffee cup into partial obscurity behind a stand of potted plants. Though her recently acquired fluency in Italian had deserted her, she could understand what was being said, and she overheard one woman say in a penetrating whisper that the new Signora Barsini might be beautiful but she had no more animation than a stuffed doll, and Cesare, who appreciated wit in women, would soon tire of her.

'Especially now the Contessa di Monticelli is widowed,' her companion suggested maliciously. 'You know she is living in Genoa and it is rumoured that he sees her every day.'

Their voices sank, but Shelagh caught the words ... 'new law' ... and 'divorce', with sly nudges and stifled laughter. So already there was gossip and conjecture about her husband and Beatrice, and Shelagh's humiliation was complete.

They drove home in silence. From time to time Shelagh was aware that Cesare glanced at her, but she did not speak. If he were going to criticise her pathetic performance at the dinner party, she would fend him off until the morning when she felt better able to cope with him. But he still did not speak when they reached the Villa, but helped her out of the car and guided her up the steps with almost tender concern, though a glance at his face showed it was cold and as impassive as marble.

At the foot of the stairs she drew away from his supporting arm, saying more sharply than she had intended: 'Thank you, I can manage without support. I'm not a cripple.'

'I never supposed you were, *mia cara,*' he returned mildly. 'But as you looked so pale and were so quiet this evening, I feared you must be feeling ill, and so I excused you to my colleagues.'

'I suppose you had to say something to cover your wife's inadequacies,' Shelagh snapped, her control slipping. Was he so insensitive that he could not realise how the scene with Rita had upset her, and then to be exposed to those sneering women's gossip for which he had given them cause. She would not plead that she had had a migraine, for she doubted the genuineness of his concern. Instead she told him:

'Let me tell you I found your friends as boring and empty-headed as they obviously found me.'

She had raised her voice in an endeavour to conceal its trembling, and he glanced round, suspecting the presence of listening servants.

'No more tonight, you're tired,' he checked her. 'If you want an inquest we will hold it in the morning. I must put the car away.'

He went back into the hall and Shelagh continued her way upstairs. How he always contrived to put her in the wrong—first she was accused of spoiling his daughter, then his dinner party, and now of provoking a slanging match within hearing of the servants. His well-bred Contessa would never be guilty of such misdemeanours. Mismated, that's what we are, she thought bitterly as she gained her room and stripped off her beautiful dress, which she had put on with such high hopes. How long would it be before Cesare approached her with the solution? But the thought of an annulment brought no comfort. Maddening, domineering, cruel even he might be, she could not bear to face the thought of life apart from him.

Shelagh awoke in the morning to find Rita sitting on the foot of her bed. She was neatly dressed in her school uniform and she looked smug.

'*Buon giorno*, Mamma,' she said cheerfully. 'Papa says I must say goodbye before I go to school. I have had breakfast with him. It was too early to wake you up, you see, and he is going to drive me to the convent. I'm going to learn how to behave like a great lady.'

Cesare had evidently been giving his daughter a lecture upon what would be expected of her, Shelagh thought, and apparently had made some impression upon her. She said a little wistfully:

'Last night you said you hated school.'

'Oh, I don't really. It's fun playing with other girls who are young like me, not old like you and Papa,' Rita said loftily. She jumped off the bed, kissed Shelagh perfunctorily, and made her a formal little curtsey. '*Ciao*, Mamma!'

She ran out of the room, leaving Shelagh feeling that even with regard to Rita she was becoming superfluous. Cesare, when he was not annoyed by her temper, had more influence with the child than she had. To become a great lady, was she in her turn to be admonished upon how far short she had fallen from that ideal?

But Cesare made no reference to that ill-fated evening beyond requesting the return of the emeralds to put in his safe. Shelagh did not see him until dinner time and during the meal he was coolly polite and seemed preoccupied. For the next few days he was rarely at home, and she wondered if he were avoiding her. With Rita at school time hung heavy on her hands, and she took to exploring the town. It presented great contrasts, modern skyscrapers rubbing shoulders with picturesque buildings in odd corners that one so often comes upon in Italy where the past still lingers. There were well designed squares and dimly lit ornate churches, in which Shelagh found the same peace and solace that she had found in the chapel at the convent so many years ago.

Returning from one of these excursions, she found her drawing room occupied by a tall brunette to whom Cesare was talking earnestly. As she came in they were sitting together on the settee, his handsome head inclined towards his visitor with an air of intimacy. They heard her before she could retreat, and the lady turned her head and smiled.

'Ah, Cesare, this must be your child bride.' She rose from her seat, advancing upon Shelagh, taking both her hands and kissing her on both cheeks. '*Mia cara*, we must be such good friends, for I have known Cesare for many, many years.'

Shelagh did not need Cesare's formal introduction, for she had guessed at once that this must be the Contessa de Monticelli. She murmured something noncommittal in answer to Beatrice's gush and Cesare rang for coffee. Child bride! she thought indignantly, what had Cesare been saying? She glanced at him reproachfully, but he was grinning wickedly, evidently amused by Beatrice's greeting.

The coffee tray was brought, and Shelagh dispensed it, while Beatrice monopolised Cesare's attention, speaking of mutual friends and shared events unknown to Shelagh, throwing an occasional word of explanation to her hostess. Thus Shelagh had plenty of opportunity to observe her. Beatrice di Monticelli was tall with a beautifully proportioned figure, every movement she made was graceful, like a lazy cat. Her dark hair was swept back under a black veil, her features were classical. Her voice was deep and musical, when amused she had a throaty, sexy laugh. Her dark eyes were big and lustrous. Everything about her was perfect, her mourning dress well cut, her crêpe veil hung elegantly, shoes and gloves were obviously expensive. She had all the assurance that Shelagh lacked, the arrogance of birth and an unassailable position—and she's hard, Shelagh thought, like a black diamond, as bright and indestructible, for all Cesare treats her as if she were some fragile plant. For his attitude as he waited upon her, handing her her coffee, settling a cushion behind her back, was tenderly protective, to Shelagh's intense annoyance. She was wondering if she could find some excuse to leave the pair together, for she felt excluded, when Cesare was called to the telephone in the next room.

'Please to amuse our guest,' he said to Shelagh. 'I shall not be long.'

'Come and sit beside me,' Beatrice besought her, patting the seat Cesare had vacated. Somewhat reluctantly Shelagh accepted her invitation. The hard black eyes studied her, and she became aware of the full force of the other woman's magnetic personality, which seemed to sap her own energies, so that she felt like a lifeless automaton.

'Let me look at you, *mia cara,*' Beatrice requested in honey-sweet tones. She spoke in English with only a trace of accent. 'How young you are! You make Cesare and me appear like old ... what do you say? ... has-beens.'

Shelagh demurred politely, thinking that neither could possibly be described as has-beens; both were still full of vitality. Beatrice's eyes roved over Shelagh's slight figure, outlined by her clinging wool dress, and her handsome mouth curled disdainfully. Her obvious contempt roused the Irish in Shelagh and she threw back her head defiantly while her green eyes sparkled irefully.

'Well, madam, having assessed me, what are your conclusions?' she asked scornfully. 'I'm not an infant, you know, I'm over twenty-one.'

'*Davvoro*, you surprise me.' Beatrice's smile did not reach her eyes. 'Forgive an old friend's curiosity, and Cesare and I are very old friends. Naturally I'm intrigued by Cesare's *third* wife. One would think that after two essays in matrimony, both ending so tragically, he would be disinclined to wed again without very strong inducement, which seems to be lacking. If he has done so for the sake of his child, he would have done better to select someone more mature.'

'Surely that is his business,' Shelagh told her frigidly.

'*D'accordo*, but ...!' The Contessa shook her head sadly. 'Men can be so weak where a designing woman is concerned.' Shelagh's eyes flashed, but the older woman continued smoothly, 'We never thought he would put anyone in Carlotta's place. He was absolutely heartbroken when she died. My husband and I knew her well and we were present at the wedding. I was unacquainted with his first wife, but that was only an absurd boy and girl affair, another mes alliance.' Shelagh winced at the dig. 'Mercifully she died giving him a son. You know he has a son?'

Shelagh nodded, relieved that apparently Cesare had not betrayed her connection with Camillo. She would hate this haughty Italian to know how he had treated her.

'He is in America, I understand?' Beatrice's arched brows expressed a query.

'I believe so.' Shelagh was determined not to be communicative.

'The little girl is Carlotta's,' the Contessa told her unnecessarily. 'Such a delightful child. Ah, poor Carlotta, she did not have her baby long. She was such a sweet creature—such elegance, such sophistication—but alas, so delicate. Cesare was so proud of her intelligence and her lineage, besides being devoted to her. I am afraid you will have a hard, in fact an impossible task to . . . er . . . step into her shoes, as you say.'

'I've no intention of trying,' Shelagh blurted out, nettled by this succession of barbed darts. The Contessa was praising her predecessor to emphasise her own inadequacies, but even she could not claim that Carlotta had been beautiful.

'But surely Cesare expects . . .?' Again the raised brows, but Shelagh said nothing. 'Such red hair,' Beatrice sighed again, studying her. 'Some people admire it, but I always think it is a little . . . outré, shall we say, to put it nicely.'

'If you mean vulgar, why don't you say so?' Shelagh retorted. 'But didn't the Venetian noblewomen have red hair?'

'*Mia cara*, you can't be compared with them,' Beatrice objected. 'They were, as you say, noblewomen.' She waved slim manicured hands expressively. 'You can imagine how astonished we all were when we learned that Cesare had married again. We believed he would mourn Carlotta all his life, but men are sadly fickle. I expected his choice would be a middle-aged lady with perhaps a handsome dowry. That would be understandable, but to elevate such a young girl, and one so naïve!' She shook her head.

'You speak as if to be young was a crime,' Shelagh cried. 'And one soon grows out of naïveté.'

'But you haven't, have you, *cara*?' Beatrice purred silkily. 'Nor become poised. No doubt Cesare found the ingénue act amusing at first, but it grows tedious with repetition, and when it comes to entertaining...' Beatrice again shook her veiled head in mock reproof. 'How Cesare's pride must have suffered!'

Shelagh flushed miserably. Cesare must have told her about that unfortunate party, and the knowledge that her husband had discussed her shortcomings with Beatrice was like a stiletto thrust in her heart.

'I can see her now,' Beatrice went on dreamily, 'seated at the head of Cesare's table, so dignified and gracious, wearing the Barsini emeralds—such a beautiful necklace; you must get Cesare to show it to you some time, it is magnificent.'

'I've worn it,' Shelagh told her, enjoying a moment of triumph.

Beatrice looked disgusted. *'Questo si che è troppo,'* she muttered.

'Of course in England we aren't so formal,' Shelagh began, meaning to excuse herself, and the Contessa interrupted her:

'That too. Was Cesare mad to marry a British girl?' The diamond-bright eyes narrowed. 'To ally himself with a *turista*!'

She uttered the last word as if it were an obscenity, and again Shelagh flushed. She knew the Italian upper classes looked askance at the freedom of foreign girls.

'No better than she should be,' the Contessa muttered, but she had gone too far.

'You're insulting, *signora*.' Shelagh's eyes flashed. 'I'm perfectly respectable, and you might reflect that though it may seem incomprehensible to you, I *am* my husband's choice, and I'm afraid he's stuck with me.'

She bit her lip, wishing she could recall that last phrase, for it implied that Cesare was having regrets, and she had no wish to expose her heartache to this woman who she was sure wanted Cesare for herself. Beatrice smiled enigmatically and Shelagh feared she was going to say he could find a way out, but instead the Contessa patted her hand and said soothingly:

'Calm yourself, *mia cara*, I didn't mean to offend you.' (Oh, didn't you, Shelagh thought; every word she had spoken had been meant to taunt.) 'I did but voice the bewilderment of Cesare's friends.'

Then to Shelagh's relief Cesare came back into the room, apologising for his prolonged absence. Beatrice stood up and went to him, laying a possessive hand upon his sleeve.

'Think nothing of it, *amico mio*. I am glad to have had this opportunity to get to know your wife. We have had . . . what you say . . . a heart-to-heart talk.' She shot a baleful glance at Shelagh. 'But now I must go. We shall all meet again *presto*, shall we not?'

Shelagh rose from the settee and endured another Judas embrace from the departing guest, and Cesare escorted her out.

Shelagh went to a mirror on the wall and with her handkerchief rubbed the spot where the Contessa's lips had touched her cheek, wishing she could as easily erase her poisonous innuendoes from her mind. The room seemed pervaded with her scent, she used something musky and exotic. Shelagh moved to open the window as Cesare came back into the room.

'Charming woman, isn't she?' he said.

'Devastatingly so,' Shelagh returned; he could have no idea of how his girl-friend had baited her. He was looking particularly bland and Shelagh had to restrain a strong urge to slap his smooth face. He was being obtuse.

'I feel as though a steamroller had passed over me,' she added.

Cesare raised his black brows interrogatively. 'What very peculiar idioms you use! You mean she had a strong personality?'

'Quite overwhelming.'

He sighed. 'I should like you two to be friends. I'm sure Bea could help you socially if you would allow yourself to be guided by her.'

That was too much! Angry spots of colour rose in Shelagh's cheeks, but controlling herself she said sweetly:

'I'm afraid that's not possible, Cesare. The Contessa and I could never see eye to eye. There's too big a gap in age.'

Cesare's face darkened and his eyes became grey ice. Only then did it occur to her that what she had said applied to him also, for he was Beatrice's contemporary.

'Oh, Cesare, I didn't mean . . .' she cried distractedly, but he was striding out of the room, and as she ran towards him, hands outstretched, he had gone through the door, very deliberately shutting it behind him.

White-faced, she stared at its panels with growing despair. His action had been symbolical. Between her and her husband there would always be a closed door.

CHAPTER EIGHT

ONE unexpected result of her encounter with Beatrice di Monticelli was a stiffening of Shelagh's morale. In spite of the Contessa's assurance and, as Shelagh feared, her increasing hold upon Cesare, she was *not* his wife, as Shelagh was, even though her claim to that position was a hollow one. Although Shelagh daily dreaded a suggestion from Cesare that their union had been a mistake and a request for his freedom, she was determined not to relinquish him without a fight. She might not possess Carlotta's advantages, but she had youth on her side, and without being vain she knew that grooming and expensive clothes had enhanced her looks. The expressions of the men she met told her that they admired her, so that if Cesare were not a fish she still hoped to break down his indifference. As for her red hair which Beatrice had so derided, she knew that Cesare appreciated it, and there had been moments like the night when he had kissed her neck when she had made some impact upon him. Unfortunately Margarita had prevented her following his lead, and after that with the disagreement over the child and her migraine the evening had turned sour. Also she was still somewhat in awe of him, it seemed almost presumption to dream that he would ever really love her.

If only she had more experience to enable her to take advantage of their life together she might win her heart's desire. But it was uphill work, for he seemed to be retreating further from her with each day that passed, and she knew it was Beatrice's influence working against her. The widow was always at the house and spent hours alone with him in the room he used as an office. Once when, stung beyond endurance, Shelagh had remarked upon the frequency of her visits, Cesare had reprimanded her, saying she ought to realise that the Contessa's affairs were very complicated, he had been appointed executor of her husband's will and as an old friend of the family it was his duty to help and sustain her all he could. He concluded his remarks by enquiring:

'You aren't by any chance jealous of Bea, are you?'

His grey eyes had looked at her penetratingly with a curious sort of eagerness, but Shelagh, quick to repudiate what she knew to be the truth, had returned emphatically:

'Certainly not! I could never be jealous of you.'

He gave a sharp sigh and told her: 'Nor would I ever give you cause.'

She hoped that was true, but she had learned that Italian men had no scruples about deceiving their wives when they were in pursuit of their pleasures.

They dined out frequently, not big affairs like the party that had so dismayed her, but more intimate gatherings with only about six or eight guests. Shelagh learned to behave with confidence and converse politely in Italian, though she lacked animation. Cesare insisted that she was always beautifully dressed and spent large sums on her clothes and hairdressing, but she did not care for his middle-aged friends and their sharp-eyed women. She was aware that Genoese society was puzzled by Cesare's marriage to her and that she was the subject of endless speculation. She suspected the universal conclusion was that 'there's no fool like an old fool'. When they were not entertaining or being entertained, Cesare usually went out in the evening, leaving her to eat alone, and she feared he went to seek more congenial company with Beatrice. The Contessa was still observing strict mourning and did not appear in public.

Shelagh's constant companion was Margarita and at weekends or on one of the innumerable saints' days that were always holidays at the convent, they would go out for the day into the hills or on to the beaches, wearing comfortable informal clothes and when the weather was fine taking a picnic basket for lunch. Sometimes Margarita brought a little friend and the trio would romp and play, recapturing Shelagh's repressed youth. A car and a chauffeur was always at their disposal, for Shelagh could not drive and Cesare did not like them going out unattended. The driver at her suggestion would betake himself to a *caffé* to play dominoes and drink wine until they were ready to go home again. That was, until Beatrice di Monticelli turned her attention to Cesare's daughter.

Shelagh had planned an expedition along the coast by train, for Rita, like so many children who have been brought up with cars, adored the novelty of travelling by train or bus. They were at breakfast, and discussing what they would do during the day, when the Contessa was shown into the room. Shelagh stared at her in surprise, as she rose to greet her, and saw her frown at their unconventional garb. As the weather was still warm, Rita was wearing shorts with a jersey, and Shelagh a sweater and slacks.

'I'm afraid my husband is out,' Shelagh informed the visitor, relieved to escape the customary embrace which Beatrice always offered when Cesare was present. He had left early for his down-town offices.

Beatrice smiled. 'I knew that, *signora*. It is for the little one I have come. Margarita, I know you have a holiday and I am going to take you to Alassio for the day. I arranged it with your papa last night.'

Rita looked mutinous. 'I was going with Mamma in the train.'

'Train? *Madonna mia,* why travel by the nasty dirty things? We will go by car and at Alassio you shall go on the sea in a boat to the Isola Gallinera. Wouldn't you like that?'

Rita looked doubtfully at Shelagh. 'I would like to go in a boat.'

'Of course you would,' the Contessa declared. 'And afterwards we will have a meal at a *ristorante,* as if you were a real grown-up lady, and I will buy you a present, a memento of our day together. But you must dress yourself properly to do me credit.'

'Can't Mamma come too?' Rita asked, allured by this glittering prospect.

'I'm sure she would prefer not to do so,' Beatrice said firmly. 'Three is such an awkward number.' She smiled falsely at Shelagh. 'Run along and change, *piccolina.* Your papa thought that you and I should become better acquainted.'

The mention of her father decided Rita. She ran to the door, crying, '*Un momento, signora.* Concetta will find my best dress.'

Swallowing her chagrin, Shelagh said: 'Surely shorts are suitable for boating?'

'They are not suitable for a Signorina Barsini,' Beatrice returned acidly. 'I do not like to be seen with *una ragazza* looking like a tramp. We know the English are casual about clothes.' She stared pointedly at Shelagh's slacks. 'But I have a position to keep up, and so has Cesare.'

Rita came back in the evening with her arms full of expensive presents, chattering excitedly about the 'Chicken Island' so called because the Romans were supposed to have introduced poultry there. She was overtired and over-stimulated and threw a tantrum when Shelagh wanted to put her to bed. Finally she was very sick, having been allowed too many sweets.

Cesare was for once in for dinner that night and Shelagh made her complaint.

'Not only did she upset all my arrangements, but she over-indulged the child. She was worn out and bilious.'

'That was unfortunate,' Cesare agreed. 'Bea is not used to children, having none of her own, but she meant to be kind. Next time I must warn her not to be so generous.'

'Next time?' Shelagh stared at him indignantly. 'You'll permit her to go out with her again?'

'But of course. Poor Bea is lonely, she has suffered a great loss, and you should be glad if she can find consolation with the little one. Surely you don't grudge her Rita's company?'

Shelagh very definitely did, for she knew Beatrice's intention was to wean Rita away from her, but she could not say that to Cesare.

'I too am lonely,' she protested.

'You don't need to be. There are plenty of people who are ready to be friendly if you weren't so aloof.'

'They aren't my sort,' she told him plaintively. 'We ... we haven't anything in common.' She looked at him wistfully. 'If only you could spare me more of your time. This is the first time you've been in to dinner this week.'

'*Mia cara*, I have our living to make,' he returned coldly. 'My work stretches beyond office hours. I have clients to entertain at night. Competition increases daily. If only Camillo ...' He broke off, biting his lip. He rarely mentioned his son and Shelagh knew he had hoped the younger man would take some of his burden off his shoulders.

'But in Venice ...' she began, thinking he had had more leisure then.

'Even a business magnate has holidays,' he pointed out. 'But most of the Venetian business has been transferred over here. In mediaeval times Venice and Genoa were great maritime rivals, but now their interests have merged. The work multiplies.' He passed his hand across his forehead. 'Also I have developed a need to distract myself.'

Or a need for excuses, Shelagh thought. Men could always screen their underhand activities with the plea of extra work. But Cesare did look tired and she said naïvely:

'Couldn't I do something to help? After all, I have worked in an office.'

He looked astonished, then laughed.

'No, no, *mia cara*, I would not ask that of you. Continue to look decorative and run my house. That is all I require of you.'

But she didn't run his house, his competent staff did that, and she had no occupation. Now it seemed even Rita was to be taken away from her—to console the Contessa! She said with inward trepidation:

'You ask so little, Cesare. I could give ... much more.'

'Could you?' His eyes slid over her assessingly, her beautifully moulded neck and shoulders revealed by her low-cut dress, her big green eyes that fell before his quizzical gaze, and the glory of her red-gold hair. A spark of flame kindled in his eyes and Shelagh felt her pulses quicken as he stood up, saying brusquely:

'You don't know what you're saying. You're so young and untouched, and I ... I'm growing old, as you've implied more than once. *Scusi*.'

They had reached the dessert, and he went abruptly out of the room, leaving a half peeled apple on his plate and his wine unfinished.

Frustrated and rejected as she was, it more than

once occurred to Shelagh that it would be more dignified to return to England and take up her former life than to remain merely tolerated in Cesare's house. That by doing so she would leave the field clear for the Contessa was a hurtful thought, but she would prefer to leave of her own accord than wait for Cesare to push her. England presented a bleak prospect. Gillian, the one friend she had kept up with, would think she was a fool to have made so little use of her opportunities, and the nuns who had reared her would consider she had failed in her duty, and be shocked that she had broken her marriage vows, however meaningless they had become. Moreover, the thought of never seeing Cesare again was desolating, in spite of her humiliations. While she remained beside him there was always a faint hope that something might happen to soften his feelings towards her. But his fine house, the luxury with which he surrounded her, her clothes and jewels were no compensation for the lack of love in her life, and if he had none to give her, should she not strive to forget him and seek it elsewhere? She shrank from making the final severance, though his absorption in the Contessa was a daily irritant, and waited for the inevitable climax to come to a head with deep foreboding, but when it did occur it was not at all what she had expected.

Christmas came and went. Shelagh bought presents for Rita and Gillian and sent cards to the nuns. Her personal commitments were pitifully small. There were plenty of other cards to be despatched in her name and Cesare's to people who were little more than names to her. She wanted to give Cesare something, but he had everything, and it would be bought with his own money, but not wishing to exclude him she bought an onyx desk set. He gave her a diamond bracelet.

The New Year was much more of a festival than Christmas in Italy. Cesare took Shelagh and Rita to Beatrice's flat on New Year's Day to wish the Contessa a happier future.

Beatrice lived in a modern block of flats and her apartment was handsomely furnished. They brought with them flowers and fruit, and Cesare presented her with a small sealed package which Shelagh surmised contained a jewel. The cream-washed walls of the sitting room were hung with gold-framed mirrors, like the hotel in Venice. They had the effect of making it seem more spacious. Mirrors seemed to play a significant part in Shelagh's impressions of Italy, and it often seemed to her that her own existence was like a reflection without depth of the life that was passing her by. Like the Lady of Shalott she watched the shadows of the world appear without participating.

Beatrice's walls showed endless replicas of the four of them. Herself in a well cut skirt and jacket with a mink stole, accepted under protest, but after all, minks were bred in captivity and not trapped; Rita in a bright woollen coat, Cesare immaculate in a perfectly tailored suit, suave and elegant as usual, and the Contessa still wearing a crêpe veil—because she knows it suits her, Shelagh thought uncharitably, a menacing figure among the bright furnishings of her room, gold and crimson brocade upholstery, and coloured Venetian glass in her cabinets. Like a black spider weaving her webs of intrigue, Shelagh's excited fancy decided, a black widow spider seeking to entrap Cesare and eliminate herself. They exchanged greetings, Beatrice bestowing the usual formal pecks on Shelagh's cheeks, then she kissed Cesare and not formally at all. Catching Shelagh's expression, she smiled and said:

'It is the custom on *il primo dell' anno.*'

But Cesare had not kissed his wife.

January was wet and cold for Italy. One gloomy day, finding the atmosphere of the villa depressing with Cesare out and Rita at school, Shelagh decided to go for a walk, ignoring the dismal drizzle in the hope that exercise would raise her spirits.

She gained the street, vaguely aware of a masculine figure standing on the opposite side of the road, regarding her intently. She walked away briskly hoping he would not follow her, having had some experience of the predatory habits of Italian males.

'Sancia!'

She stopped as if shot. Only one person had called her that and a surge of memories washed over her. The sunlit beaches of Venezia, the brief flowering of love and ecstasy. Slowly she turned round and saw the young man coming towards her, arms outstretched.

'Sancia, baby!'

'Camillo!

Too astonished to resist, she allowed him to embrace her. His lips sought hers, hot and hungry, but no answering flame was lit in her. His physical attraction for her was dead, she realised with relief. With flaming cheeks she hurriedly extricated herself.

'Cam, how dare you! Here in the street!'

Luckily the rain had driven possible spectators indoors.

He smiled, his familiar devastating smile. 'Still a little prude? Baby, you always turned me on. I couldn't help myself.' She noticed an American twang had become imposed on his Italian accent, and it was not an improvement. 'I must talk to you,' he went on. 'It's important.'

She shook her head, recalling all he had caused her to suffer.

'I've nothing to say to you, Cam, not now or at any time.'

She moved to walk on, but he caught hold of her arm.

'Aw, come on, baby. No way you can walk out on me. I need your help.'

'Me walk out on you?' she laughed bitterly.

'Are you still sore at me?' He seemed surprised. 'Of course dear Pop will have spun you a yarn, and I bet he made me out a scab.'

He shivered. The cheap smart overcoat he wore was not much protection against the rain which was beginning to come down hard. Shelagh's white raincoat and hood was much more serviceable.

'Come on, lovely,' he urged, 'let's go where we can natter, and I'll tell you what really happened. You'll flip.'

The pseudo Americanisms jarred, but his tone was wheedling and his expressive dark eyes were openly admiring. Shelagh was bored and it was pleasant to be appreciated after Cesare's cold courtesy. It might even be amusing to learn how Camillo would endeavour to excuse his appalling conduct and he had no power now to hurt her. She was not above a faint curiosity as to her successor, for Cesare had told her another woman had been involved.

'Very well, I'll have a coffee with you,' she agreed. 'But I can't be away long.'

Retaining a possessive hold on her arm, Camillo guided her into a side street where an ultra-modern red sports car was parked. She stared at it in surprise; at least he was not broke, unless it was stolen. She wouldn't put that past him either. A reckless mood took hold of her; she had nothing to lose by this adventure and it would while away the long dull afternoon.

Camillo drove fast out of the town with the usual rash impetuosity of Italian drivers, who are among the worst in the world. Shelagh began to wonder if all her problems might be solved by a head-on crash. From time to time she glanced at the man beside her; he was stouter, and his handsome features had coarsened, but he was still recognisable as the charming youth who had so beguiled her. His profile was like his father's except for the weakness of his chin, and his long sideboards emphasised his Latin appearance. His curly black hair was long enough to cover his ears, and there were several flashy rings on his long brown fingers.

He drew off the autostrada at an interjunction with a screech of tyres and drove down a byroad towards the sea, pulling up with a squeal of brakes outside a *pasticceria* where coffee and cakes could be obtained. He sprang out of his seat and opened her door with a flourish, a gleam of white teeth and an inclination of his black head.

'*Avanti, carissima!*'

'You're as dramatic as an actor,' she said disdainfully as he helped her out of the low seat.

'Funny you should say that,' he observed. 'That's what I am.'

'Really?'

'I'll tell you presently.'

They entered the *pasticceria,* which was dimly lighted with partitions between the tables. Evidently Camillo knew the place. Choosing a secluded corner, he ordered coffee and pastries which arrived with commendable promptitude, paying Shelagh fulsome compliments while they waited. She was looking lovelier than ever, she had acquired such an air, such style, without losing any of her youthful charm.

'Now,' she said, when the waitress had served them, 'cut the soft soap and explain yourself.'

She was sitting opposite to him and her green gaze met his dark eyes levelly. For the first time he showed a faint embarrassment, turning away his head.

'Honey, no way are you going to believe this.'

'Try me,' she suggested uncompromisingly.

He flashed her his brilliant smile. 'Actually I've come to make it up with the old man,' he said bluntly. 'After all, I'm his only son until you oblige.' His insolent gaze slid down her slim figure and Shelagh blushed. 'I hoped you'd persuade him to forgive me.'

'Why should I?' Shelagh asked coldly.

'Because you're an adorable girl and don't bear malice,' Camillo informed her. 'You loved me once. If you'll point out to Pop that I'm the prodigal son and all that...' He gesticulated.

'Can't you do that yourself?'

'I wrote to him a while back, but he didn't answer.'

'I'm not surprised,' Shelagh remarked, reflecting that Cesare had never mentioned this approach. She held up her hand as Camillo started to pour out a torrent of American-Italian speech condemning Cesare's hard heart.

'Have you no shame, Cam? Your behaviour was despicable and he is an honourable man. You hurt him, and he wasn't the only one who was hurt.' She looked at him reproachfully. 'What about me?'

'Aw, baby, I wouldn't have hurt you for the world,' Camillo exclaimed ardently. 'You don't understand. What I did was all done for you.'

'Oh, really, Cam!' Shelagh exclaimed in disgust, and made to rise from the table. She had had enough of Camillo, who, she suspected, had returned to try to extract money from his father, and his last statement was outrageous. He put his hand over hers on the table to restrain her, saying urgently:

'No, listen, listen! You believe I was unfaithful to you, but it was not so.'

'Oh, all right, Cam.' Shelagh subsided in her seat.

'I'm listening, but you'll need to make it good to convince me.'

'While you were away, I met this American in Portofino. She was an actress—resting, as they say.'

'Of course,' Shelagh nodded. 'And she was beautiful? And kind?'

'Damn it all,' Camillo exploded. 'What if she was? Was it a sin to admire her? The point is she admired *me*. She said I was the most handsome young man she had ever met. I had the face and charm of a second Valentino. All I needed was the opportunity.'

'Which she offered?' Shelagh asked sweetly, beginning to be revolted by the smug self-satisfaction Camillo exuded.

'It was business, only business between us,' Camillo declared. 'I swear that, honey.' His English began to become less grammatical, and he gesticulated violently with his hands. 'We talk and talk. When she go back to America she want me to join her, but I think of you, *bambina*.' His limpid black eyes gazed at Shelagh with amorous intensity. 'I tell her we are about to be married. I cannot leave you, and she say, perhaps later, but then, *presto*, she has the chance of a lifetime, a fantastic part in a major film, and if I go with her she will make me a star. But there is no time. If I do not go with her all will be lost. I feel I *must* go.' He dropped his voice and for the first time a note of sincerity came into his voice. 'I never wanted to be a business man. Sitting at a desk, dealing with shipping orders, manifestos, bills of lading—ugh!' He spread his hands. 'It is not me. I have the chance to become rich and famous. It is the life I was meant for, and...' He gazed at her beseechingly. 'It was all for you I meant to return and lay it all at your feet, together with myself.'

The false note of theatricality jarred upon Shelagh as his Americanisms did. Camillo was phoney right through and even a fool would know what his relations with his 'friend' must have been. She made a small sound of dissent, but he went on imperviously.

'Believe me, baby, at that moment in time it was imperative that I go before the old man find out, for he would have stopped me going. But when I think of you coming to Venice I feel my heart will break. My friend, understands I love you only. She says if you love me you not want to stand in my way.'

'If all this is true,' Shelagh said coldly, unmoved by the appeal in his dark eyes, 'you could have let me know and we could have postponed the wedding.'

'Sancia, I dare not. I would have to give a reason and if you told Pop, he would have stopped me, as he has always stopped me doing what I wanted to do. There was no time. I had to leave at once.'

'Yet you found time to write me a note to say you couldn't meet me.'

'I thought you would realise something tremendous had happened,' Camillo said glibly. 'Only an earth-shaking event would keep me from you. I couldn't miss that chance. I was sure that when I returned rich and famous you would forgive me, but...' He looked at her accusingly. 'You did not wait.'

'And have you returned rich and famous?' Shelagh asked, ignoring his reproach.

Camillo looked slightly dashed. 'Not exactly,' he admitted. 'My friend let me down. There was no part for me, she wanted ... but I'll not offend your ears with her squalid importunities.' Shelagh nearly laughed at this sudden assumption of prudery. 'You see, I was true to you. But I am doing very well, I'm a top model. I pose for advertisements and my time will come to star in films. Meanwhile I make good money.'

'I'm glad to hear that,' Shelagh said, wondering what she had ever seen in Camillo Barsini. The young man was eaten up with vanity, a shallow self-seeker. Extraordinary that he should be Cesare's son, but Cesare had said his mother had been empty-headed and Giovanna had spoilt him in infancy with this result. 'Why are you here?' she added, for if he had no need to beg there seemed no reason for his presence.

'How can you ask?' he demanded with a languorous glance out of long-lashed eyes that had once seemed so alluring and now repelled her. 'I am on an assignment in Rome. I flew up to catch a glimpse of my beloved.'

Shelagh raised her hand. 'None of that, Cam. All that was between us was over when I married your father.'

Camillo grinned. 'I was sure he'd look after you, but you can't pretend you love him, surely? Not like we did.'

'Certainly not like we did,' Shelagh agreed. There was no similarity between the deep love and gratitude she felt towards Cesare and her brief infatuation with this spoilt, conceited youth seated opposite to her. 'But he was very deeply incensed by your behaviour and I see no likelihood of effecting a reconciliation. Please leave us alone, Cam. We're ... happily married.' Camillo was quick enough to note the slight catch in her voice and stored it for future reference. 'I suggest you take the next plane back to Rome and get on with the life you've chosen.'

'Aw, come off it, baby,' Camillo drawled, becoming very American. 'I came in my car anyway, and you don't have to put on an act with me. I don't blame you for accepting the old man, you hadn't much option, but there's no need to pretend to be a devoted wife. I've come back to you, *carissima,* don't you understand? We can be together again. You've become a wow, Sancia, a real wow, well worth waiting for.'

'Please don't talk like that,' Shelagh said sharply. 'Have you forgotten you're my stepson?'

Camillo looked so taken aback that it was obvious he had been too taken up with his own reactions to consider their present relationship with all its implications. Actually it had only just occurred to Shelagh.

'Dio mio!' he exclaimed, and began to laugh. *'Mia matrigna!* How fantastic!'

'It is, isn't it?' Shelagh agreed, 'but it's true.'

'Mia piccola matrigna,' Camillo repeated, amorousness giving place to sentimentality, so that Shelagh marvelled at the versatility of his feelings. 'That sure makes you something special. When first I saw you I was overwhelmed by memories of Venezia and I clean forgot you're one of the family. Now you must persuade Pop to forgive me so we can all be one happy family together.'

Shelagh sighed. 'It's not as easy as that, Cam.'

His eyes narrowed cunningly. 'There's one big, black fly in the ointment, is that not so?'

'What do you mean?'

'Aw, baby, be your age. Naturally I've kept tabs on Pop, and Genoese gossip reaches as far as Rome. Bea di Monticelli is widowed, isn't she, and Pop follows her like her shadow.'

Shelagh put her hand over her mouth to conceal her trembling lips. So Cesare's attentions to Beatrice were common knowledge, and Camillo knew her marriage was threatened. He went on reflectively:

'Come to think of it, poor Pop's had a bit of a raw deal. First my mother dying when I was born and then that wet Carlotta d'Este wished on to him by my grandfather, who was alive then and persuaded him it was his duty to marry her and get her money. I don't suppose he grieved much when she died.' (A very different story from Beatrice's.) 'He's been hankering after Bea for years, and now she's free he's tied himself up with you. Crazy, isn't it?'

'It was very noble of him . . .' Shelagh began, anxious to defend Cesare.

'He got some fun out of it, didn't he?' Camillo said coarsely. 'But Bea would be a much more suitable wife for him, she's nearer his age.' He frowned thoughtfully. 'I daresay he'd jump at a divorce if you asked him for one and he'd make a very generous settlement to compensate you. Don't worry, little stepmother, I'll take you to America and with what he gives you we can set up in business. You've the face and figure to make a good model, and between us we should be able to earn plenty.' He smiled at her with all his old winning charm. 'I'll look after you, baby.'

'That's big of you,' Shelagh observed sarcastically. 'You did it so well before, didn't you?'

'Aw, baby, let that rest. I've explained how it came about,' he said easily, as if his improbable story had justified his conduct. 'We must think of the future now.'

'A future in which you've no part, Cam,' Shelagh told him firmly, and he laughed again, not believing her. She stood up. 'I must go back now, if you don't mind. Rita will be coming home from school.'

'My dear little sister! How I'd love to see her again.'

'Rubbish,' she returned vigorously. 'You know there's no love lost between you and her.'

He was about to protest, but the waitress came up with the bill. While he paid it, Shelagh studied him thoughtfully, realising what an escape she had had. Today she had been seeing Camillo Barsini as he really was, and she had not liked what she saw. Perhaps if guided by a stronger character, he might have been different, but nothing could shake his colossal self-conceit. The waitress was looking at him coquettishly and he was ogling her, basking in her evident admiration.

'You're incorrigible, Cam,' Shelagh said as they regained the car.

'What have I done now?' he asked, wide-eyed with an innocent little boy look. 'I can't help it if girls look at me with bedroom eyes. That one's a proper minx.'

'You know her, then?'

'Do you blame me if I look for consolation when I'm denied my own home?' He looked pathetic.

Shelagh nearly said, whose fault is that, but merely shrugged. Perhaps Camillo could not help being irresponsible.

He repeated his reckless progress back to the centre of the town, while Shelagh debated whether she would mention his reappearance to Cesare or not. If only she could be sure that he would go back to Rome, it might be better not, but she doubted that such was his intention.

As he pulled up at the kerb a few yards from the house, they saw Cesare and Beatrice standing on the steps about to enter the hall. They were so deep in conversation that they had not yet opened the door. Cesare's proud head was bent solicitously towards the Contessa and her hand was within the crook of his arm.

'You see, rumour does not lie,' Camillo said triumphantly, as he opened the car door for Shelagh. Perturbed, she stepped out on to the pavement and before she was aware of his intention, Camillo took her in his arms and imprinted a fervent kiss on her lips.

'A salute for *mia matrigna*,' he said with a wicked grin, as he released her.

Shelagh glanced nervously towards the front door, but Cesare and the Contessa had disappeared. If they had seen Camillo, surely they would have stayed? She feared he would insist upon coming in with her, but to her relief he waved his hand with a casual, 'Be seeing you,' and re-entering his car roared away.

As she let herself in by the front door, Shelagh decided that she would tell Cesare at once that his son was in Genoa. The young man evidently meant to see her again and she would hate Cesare to imagine she had been meeting the prodigal in secret. She would tell him now that Camillo had come home and wanted to be forgiven, and it would be up to him to do as he thought fit regarding him. She looked into the *salotto*, but it was empty. Cesare must be closeted with Beatrice in his private sanctum on the plea of discussing business. Respecting his privacy, it was a room she never entered when he was in it. She lingered irresolutely in the hall, wondering how long the Contessa intended to stay. She took off her raincoat, dropping it on one of the hard chairs with which the place was furnished. If she went upstairs, she might miss Cesare.

The Barsinis' Genoese house was a large edifice, a one-time *palazzo* that had been modernised. The front door was flush with the street, but most of the windows looked out at the back where the ground fell away towards the sea. There was no garden, but a paved terrace decorated with urns filled with plants made a pleasant place to sit in summer. The entrance hall was large, marble-paved, and accommodated the imposing staircase. Shelagh always thought it was more like the vestibule of a hotel than the nucleus of a home.

She waited with increasing impatience. She did not want to tell her news in front of the Contessa. Then a little spurt of anger flared up in her. This was supposed to be her house and Cesare was nominally her husband. To hell with the Contessa! She would go to his office and demand to speak to him alone.

Filled with resolution, she marched across the hall,

through an arched entry to the side of the stairs that gave access to the passage leading to Cesare's office. Her rubber-soled shoes made no sound as she traversed the corridor, and she knocked loudly on the closed door. She thought she heard a scuffle and what sounded like a stifled laugh, and her anger grew. Business indeed! What were they up to, those two, when they believed she was out of the way?

Calling, 'It's I, Shelagh, and I've news for you!' she wrenched the door ajar and stood frozen on its threshold by what she saw.

Cesare was holding Beatrice in his arms and her hands were clasped behind his neck. Her crêpe veil lay in a heap on the floor, and her rich black hair cascaded over them both, reaching nearly to her waist. The bodice of her dress was undone and her eyes were closed, the long lashes sweeping her pale cheeks. Her mouth was half open and on her face was a look of ecstasy.

Talk and surmises are one thing, they have to be proven, but an actual visual image makes a convincing impact. Shelagh knew than that all her worst conjectures were only too true.

CHAPTER NINE

For the space of a couple of breaths, Shelagh stared at the locked figures of Beatrice and her husband, while all her half-formed dreams and hopes crumbled about her. Cesare was in love with the Contessa, had always been in love with her, and his present wife was an encumbrance of which he would only be too glad to rid himself if he could do so with honour. He showed no sign of embarrassment at her intrusion. His eyes met Shelagh's over the drooping Beatrice with the coldness of a grey sea under a cloudy sky. From his expression he was consumed by the icy anger which she had always dreaded, but he was the one at fault, not herself, and she returned his stare defiantly. Later she would feel all the anguish of betrayal, but at that moment she was conscious only of outrage. That Cesare could conduct his amours under the same roof that sheltered her was insulting. He could at least confine his ardour to the Contessa's flat. Not that he was looking at all ardent, only coldly furious.

'Bea has fainted,' he said curtly. 'Be so good as to fetch a glass of water while I carry her into the *salotto*.'

He lifted the Contessa's by no means insubstantial weight in his arms with ease, and as he brushed past her, Shelagh sensed the suppressed violence in him, only partially concealed. He was not as cool as he was trying to appear. She sped kitchenwards in search of some of the staff. Cesare had been quick to explain an awkward situation, but Shelagh was not deceived. She did not believe that Beatrice had fainted. She had seen the smug complaisant smile on the Contessa's lips to find herself where she wanted to be, and her disordered clothing was proof positive of what had been happening, or so it seemed to her. Cesare had not even bothered to lock the door, and one of the maids might easily have discovered them. But perhaps the servants all knew what was going on? Shelagh felt that her heart was breaking with humiliation and woe. She found a maid and told her to take a tumbler and carafe of water to the *salotto*, searching the pert face and knowing black eyes as she gave her order, wondering what the girl was thinking. Italians loved intrigue, especially erotic intrigue, and no doubt her staff had been following their master's affair with avid interest.

As she made her way to the staircase, for she needed the sanctuary of her own room, Rita came bounding in full of high spirits.

'Papa at home?' she asked, hearing voices from the half closed door of the *salotto*.

'Yes, but the Contessa is with him. She ... isn't very well. Go to Concetta, darling, she'll see about your tea. I ... I've a headache.'

'Is everybody ill?' Rita demanded loudly, and Cesare heard her.

'Come here, *piccolina*,' he called. 'The Contessa would like to see you, but please be quiet.'

Rita went with alacrity. The arrival of Beatrice meant a present, and though she was not very fond of her, she enjoyed her bounty.

Shelagh went upstairs reflecting sourly that Beatrice's campaign to alienate Rita was progressing. Perhaps it was just as well, for she would soon be on her way out. Reaching her room, she sat down at the dressing table staring at her reflection. The mirror showed a white face, devoid of expression, like a mask with two black-ringed eyes looking through. Slowly her anger ebbed away. After all, what she had seen merely corroborated what she had known for a long time. Camillo's words reiterated through her brain.

'He's been hankering after Bea for years and now she's free, he's tied himself up with you.'

Ever since Tommaso di Monticelli had died Cesare must have been bitterly regretting his quixotic marriage to herself, and Beatrice was in every way a much more suitable partner for him—Camillo again. He had not yet suggested an annulment, it sounded so much better than a divorce, which was still frowned upon in Italy in some quarters, and perhaps he would shrink from a fourth marriage. But it was obvious he was deeply involved with the Contessa, and it was possible he depended upon his wife's presence as a smoke screen for the benefit of his friends, who she felt sure were not deceived. Camillo had told her gossip had reached as far as Rome. Being herself fundamentally honest and straightforward, her whole being revolted from the invidious position in which she was being placed. Cesare, outwardly acting the affectionate husband and in private neglecting her; herself an object of pity to her own staff, and secretly yearning for the unattainable.

The lovely room was reflected in the triple glass. The white bed was behind her, with the thin drapery hanging from the gilded crown. An exotic piece of furniture—wasn't it significant that Cesare housed her in luxury and was always giving her presents to atone for his lack of fidelity? Or could a man be unfaithful to a wife who was not a wife? Her thoughts returned to Beatrice with morbid curiosity. What did she look like in bed with all that gorgeous hair spraying the pillow? Should she ask Cesare? His reaction might be—interesting. Being an Italian she would naturally be passionate—and Cesare? Always so cool and self-possessed as he was, she could not imagine him in the throes of love. The only strong emotion he had shown in her presence was anger, and even that was always restrained. She wondered if Beatrice had recovered from her 'faint' and if she were still in the house. Suddenly she sickened of the whole miserable coil. She was out of her element here among these subtle Latins. Her best course was to return to her own country as soon as possible, and she was certain Cesare would hail her departure with relief. He might hesitate to throw her out himself, having promised to protect her, but he would be thankful if she went of her own accord.

She had nobody in England to whom to return, but the convent would give her shelter as it had taken in her mother in her hour of need. It was the nearest approach to a home she had ever known. She had feared the Sisters might censure her if she left her husband, but if she explained the situation to Mother Cecilia, who was so understanding and so wise, she did not think she would upbraid her. The Mother Superior, though she must be getting very old, was still there. Shelagh had heard from her at Christmas, and she knew she could rely upon her kind tolerance. In the tranquillity of the cloister she would find the solace her battered spirit needed so badly, and surely she could fill some humble position in a lay capacity to earn her keep? She rose from her seat and walked to the window overlooking the town where the lights were pricking the winter dusk, and saw instead in her mind's eye the grey stone walls of the convent buildings set in the green English countryside with their promise of shelter and peace.

Concetta knocked on her door, exclaimed when she saw the room was in darkness and switched on the light. She had come to say that the Signorina Margarita was having her supper and wanted the Signora to say goodnight to her. Signor Barsini had taken the Contessa home but would be back in time for dinner.

That surprised Shelagh, but she felt she could not possibly face her husband over the dinner table. She told the maid that she had a headache and would not be coming downstairs again. No, she did not want any dinner. Would she ask the cook to send up a cup of soup? She would go to bed early. 'And inform Signor Barsini,' she concluded.

Concetta nodded sympathetically with a knowing gleam in her black eyes, and Shelagh writhed inwardly. She thinks I'm showing my displeasure over my husband's concern for the Contessa, she thought. Oh, to be in England, away from all of them!

Since going to school, Rita kept more suitable hours, no longer sitting up for late dinner. Shelagh had arranged that, and Cesare since he was so often out, made no demur. Rita had been a little rebellious at first, but soon became accustomed to the new régime and was much better for it.

Shelagh went to the child's room and found Rita already in bed hugging a peculiar-looking animal with a long nose.

'It's a Womble,' Rita informed her. 'And it's from England. Zia Beatrice got it for me. Isn't she kind?'

'Very kind,' Shelagh agreed, hoping Beatrice would keep up her generosity when she had gone.

'But I like you best,' Rita, declared winding her arms about Shelagh's neck. 'You're my *mamma* and she's only a *zia*.'

Not even that, Shelagh thought, but she might become another mother. She felt a pang at the thought of leaving the child, but children grew up so quickly and Rita would still have her father, whom she adored.

Cesare apparently accepted her excuse, for no message came requesting her to come down to dinner, which she had half feared. She suspected he no more wanted to face her than she did him. She wondered why he had not stayed with the Contessa, then she dismissed him from her mind. She felt calmed, much happier now that she had made her decision. Tomorrow she would write to Mother Cecilia explaining her position, and she was confident she would not refuse her sanctuary.

She drank the soup that was brought up to her as requested, had a leisurely bath and sought her bed, the wide, soft bed that had been designed for marital transports. She smiled a little wryly as she thought of the narrow convent bedsteads with their hard mattresses. Austerity would take a little getting used to, but she would welcome it if it brought her peace of mind. Resolutely she turned her mind away from Cesare. She had learned to love him, but he did not want her love and it was no use repining. It was as simple as that.

She was dreaming of green fields and softly falling rain, when she was brought wide awake by a sudden blaze of light, as someone pressed the electric light switch. She saw to her astonishment that Cesare had come into her room. Thinking that she must still be dreaming, she sat up, blinking the sleep out of her eyes. Her hair tumbled about her shoulders, which were barely concealed by her thin nylon nightdress. The only times her husband entered her room were before an evening out when he came to give his approval to her toilette, or to collect the emeralds to put in his safe. Never before had he intruded when she was in bed. She saw that he had taken off his jacket and was in his shirt sleeves, his hair was ruffled and he looked a little—wild was the description that occurred to her. Cesare wild? Completely uncharacteristic. She wondered for a moment if he had been drinking, but she had never seen him the worse for alcohol.

'Is anything wrong?' she asked uneasily, aware of tension in the air.

'Ask your conscience that,' he returned. 'Are you a coward as well as a deceiver? These headaches of yours are your usual refuge when events become too much for you.'

He must be referring to that first dinner party when her migraine had been her excuse. She had thought it was all past and forgotten, but these Italians were a vengeful lot. Their history was full of feuds and vendettas that were never allowed to die.

'I've never deceived you,' she said quietly.

He came up to the bed and with a sudden savage movement tore down the flimsy curtaining that draped it.

'Don't lie!'

Her temper rose. She was not a coward and his senseless action was a piece of vandalism.

'I never lie,' she flashed, 'and I think you must be drunk, to behave as you're doing.'

'I'm perfectly sober. Your deceit has infuriated me.'

'You're a nice one to talk about deceit!' She was as angry as he was. 'Do you think I'm blind to what's going on? Don't tell me your Beatrice really fainted. I just walked in at the wrong moment.'

If she had not been so startled by his sudden appearance in her room and his unprecedented violence, she would not have spoken as she had done. She was resigned to the inevitable and had not meant to mention Beatrice.

'You will please not to speak of her,' he said sternly. 'You're not fit to wipe her shoes. Actually she was genuinely overcome. An old friend who didn't know of his death had written to Tommaso, and the sight of the letter which I had been holding for her overcame her. She was a very devoted wife.'

Shelagh did not believe Beatrice was so sensitive and she was certainly consoling herself. The perverse imp that had taken possession of her prompted her to say:

'A most ingenious fabrication, but you can't gull me. Why have you come home? Shouldn't you have stopped with her to continue the sympathetic treatment?'

'Because she's not my wife, and you are, though you seem to have forgotten it.'

The inimical look in his grey eyes caused her to quail in spite of her anger. His glance lingered over her slight form and creamy shoulders with such avidity that she instinctively drew the sheet up to her chin.

'Such modesty,' he sneered. 'You who embrace strange men brazenly in the street. You've told me my respectable friends bore you, so you go out and pick up riff-raff to amuse you. I trusted you, gave you my name to protect you, my honour into your keeping.'

She stared at him blankly; all recollection of the earlier events of the afternoon had been washed away by her discovery in his office.

'You're talking like someone out of a Victorian novel, Cesare. I've always been most circumspect.'

Then he struck her across the face with the back of his hand. She was so appalled that she cowered back on her pillows, still clutching the sheet, her green eyes wide and scared like a frightened cat. A devil seemed to have entered into Cesare. His pupils were enlarged by passion so that his eyes looked black. Two pieces of his rumpled hair stood up like horns, and his face was distorted by a satanic expression. He was a complete stranger, bearing no resemblance to the suave courteous Cesare she knew. Shelagh gave a little whimper and her hand went to her mouth where the ring he wore had cut her lip. Cesare smiled and his smile was more dreadful than his frown. So might one of the Borgias have looked when watching the death throes of one of their victims.

'You may think yourself lucky to live in this day and age. A couple of centuries ago and I'd have thrashed you until your back was raw.'

'But what have I done?' she cried in bewilderment.

'Don't prevaricate. I saw you with my own eyes this afternoon embracing that young jackanapes with the red sports car, who'll be seeing you soon, you shameless slut!'

She had forgotten all about Camillo. So he *had* seen her with his son, but *he had not recognised him.*

'Oh, I can explain about that,' she said, and wondered if she could. Would Cesare be placated to learn that the young jackanapes was his renegade son? Wouldn't he condemn her for going out with him? She had no idea how he felt about Camillo, whom he never mentioned. The vindictive Italian in him might make it impossible for him to forgive him, and Camillo's desertion was the initial cause of the present impasse.

'I don't want to hear your explanations,' Cesare declared. 'They would only be another pack of lies.' He moved away from the bed, prowling round the room like a predatory panther. 'Shelagh, I have given you every consideration, pampered you, striven to make you happy. I denied myself because I knew your attitude to me was to regard me as paternal. I feared my passion might frighten you, you seemed so young, so untouched, so I've waited for you to mature, only to be made a fool of.'

Shelagh uttered an incoherent murmur. He could not mean what he was saying, or did he? Had he really suffered the same frustration that had made her own life almost unbearable? She sat up in the bed, her eyes wide and eager.

'Cesare...' she breathed.

He halted beside her and looked at her scornfully.

'Are you ready to welcome me now to save yourself from something worse?' he demanded. 'You're not really innocent, are you? You're one of those modern permissive girls your country breeds nowadays. You came here hunting with that bitch of a friend of yours and you entrapped my son. He discovered what you were and so he left you. And I was an unmitigated idiot and picked up his leavings!'

He was lashing himself into even greater fury and Shelagh winced inwardly under his distorted statements. There was just enough truth in them to make them sound plausible. She did not know how to begin to refute them, nor was she given the chance. He ripped the sheet away from her clutching fingers and stared down at her quivering body with distended nostrils and smouldering eyes.

'So lovely and so frail!' he exclaimed. 'But before I thrust you out, you little cheat, you shall give me some satisfaction.'

Bravely she tried to protest:

'Cesare, let me speak, you've got it all wrong...'

'*Silenzio!*' he snarled. 'There have been too many words.'

'Please, Cesare...' she pleaded. Much as she longed for him she did not want to be taken like this, in anger instead of love, as a sort of punishment for crimes she had not committed.

'You're still my wife,' he said thickly. 'And I have rights that have been denied too long.'

With heavy hands he pressed her back on her pillows and let his weight come down upon her. He gathered up her hair in both hands, twisting it into a rope and winding it round her throat so that for one awful moment she thought he meant to strangle her, but he changed his posture to enfold her shoulders with a grip that hurt and buried his face against her breasts.

There was a sudden commotion in the passage outside the room. Someone knocked loudly on the door and a voice recognisable as that of Guido, Cesare's valet, cried: *'Signore! Signore! La polizia!'*

'Dannazione!' Cesare swore. For a moment he lay inert, then he rolled off the bed and adjusted his clothing. He crossed to the dressing table, breathing hard, and smoothed his hair with Shelagh's hair brush.

The knocking became more imperative, punctuated by excited Italian and a shaking of the door. Cesare had locked it when he came in.

'Basta,' Cesare called. *'Vengo presto!'* He looked towards the girl on the bed, with an ominous glitter in his eyes. 'This is only a temporary reprieve. There will be another night, *mia bella.*'

He walked to the door, unlocked it, extracted the key and slipped it in his pocket. He did not intend to leave her the means to keep him out.

Opening the door, he was met by a babble of shrill exclamations and explanations. All the staff seemed to be there. The words '*disgrazia*' and '*incidente*' were audible, but the still trembling Shelagh did not heed them.

'Get you all downstairs!' Cesare thundered, and all became quiet except for the sound of their retreating footsteps.

Shelagh lay still, too shocked and bruised to care what had happened. Her cheek still smarted where Cesare had struck her. She felt as a child would feel if someone it had trusted suddenly turned into a monster. Whatever had occurred had stopped Cesare from

... consummating their marriage. But what a way to set about it! She had created fantasies in which Cesare had come to her in love, but she had never imagined such fierce passion as that which had terrified her. He had seemed quite capable of killing her. She could not decide whether he had been motivated by jealousy or merely outrage that she had flouted convention. The older Italians were very strict about their wives' behaviour, however much latitude they allowed themselves, but neither were sufficient excuse for such savagery. It seemed there were depths in Cesare that she had not suspected, a primitive ferocity completely at variance with his normal civilised manner.

It occurred to her then that if Cesare had seen her with Camillo, Beatrice had been with him and must have also witnessed their parting. The Contessa would have done her best to fan his wrath, casting aspersions upon Shelagh's character. She thought she could trace the accusation of past permissiveness to her. If she had succeeded in rousing the fury which he had sought to vent upon her, she had cause to feel faint, Shelagh thought grimly, and her smug smile had been caused by contemplation of the retribution that would shortly fall upon the supposed erring wife.

She's always been out to make trouble between us, Shelagh thought wearily, and became aware of an intense thirst. Gingerly she got out of bed, slipping on her wrapper and slippers, and went into the bathroom to get a drink. She drank thirstily although the tap water was not considered very wholesome, then tiptoeing to the door she opened it cautiously and listened. The upper floor was deserted, but she could hear voices in the hall, and a sudden wail from one of the women. A shiver of premonition ran up her spine, and the words she had heard returned to her with sudden meaning. There had been an accident, possibly a serious one, but who connected with the family could have been involved at this time of night? Rita? She flew along the passage to the child's room, but Rita lay peacefully asleep undisturbed by all the racket, nursing her Womble. Shelagh left her and ran downstairs. The servants were congregated in the hall, whispering, and glancing through the archway that led to Cesare's office.

'The policeman is still here?' she asked.

'*Si, signora,*' they chorused.

'What has happened?'

They all started to gabble at once, but became quiet as Guido came along the passage. He looked pale and shaken, and Shelagh repeated her question to him.

'A man has been killed in a motor accident,' he told her.

Puzzled, she enquired, 'Was it just outside? Why should they come here?'

'They had to let *il Maestro* know.' He moistened his lips. 'It was the young *signor* who went to America. It seems he had come back, and...' He waved his hands expressively.

A red sports car that went like a bomb. Shelagh sat down abruptly on one of the hard wooden chairs.

'You said he was dead?' she whispered tonelessly.

'*Si, signora.* The car went through a wall above an embankment. The *signor* was thrown out, but the car caught fire, there is nothing left of it. *Il signor* died in the ambulance without regaining consciousness. He was identified by his papers.'

'Thank you, Guido,' she said mechanically.

The man looked compassionately at her white face, her pallor accentuated by the dark wrap she wore, and her red-gold hair hanging tangled over her shoulders.

'Would you like a drink? Or to lie down?' he asked.

'No, thank you, I'm all right. I'll wait for your master.'

So Camillo was dead, and only that afternoon she had seen him so full of life and had been repelled by him. The suddenness of it appalled her. If she had known she would have been more friendly, but how could she have foreseen it, or he either? At least they had parted with a kiss. She was glad of that now. 'Be seeing you.' But she would never see him again. Death had wiped away all his follies and pretensions. She could think of him kindly now.

Cesare. How had his father taken it? Would he grieve? She waited anxiously for him to appear. He came at last, escorting a man in uniform to the front door. He frowned when he saw the hovering servants and harshly ordered them back to bed. His face was pale and drawn, all the fire had gone out of him, and his shoulders were bowed. He looked like an old man. The officer went out into the street and Cesare locked and bolted the door behind him. Someone, Guido probably, had given him his jacket, and he appeared an entirely different person from the passionate man who had flung himself upon Shelagh's bed. He saw her as he came back from the front door, staring at him apprehensively, and he stopped in front of her.

'He wrote to me,' he told her. 'But I didn't answer his letter. Would to God I had! He must have come back intending to see me—but he's gone before we could meet.'

Shelagh stood up and laid a tentative hand on his arm.

'Come into the *salotto*, Cesare, and I'll give you a drink. You need one.'

He submitted to her guidance like a child. She seated him in an armchair and poured a stiff whisky from the tray of drinks left there from the previous evening and not yet cleared away. He drank it straight off and a little colour came back into his wan face.

'He was my only son,' he said, looking up at her but not appearing to see her. 'The last of my family.' He smiled with the ghost of his old sardonic humour. 'Not much to be proud of, perhaps, but my own flesh and blood.' He sighed. 'He was such a charming little boy. Pity he ever grew up.'

He was recalling past associations, a procession of mental pictures of the deceased. Shelagh had not thought he could grieve for Camillo, whom he had disowned. As if he had caught her thought, he said:

'I never really believed we would never meet again. I hoped he would make a decent life in America, though I've no idea what he was doing. It is possible he might have reformed.'

Shelagh reflected that it was as well he did not know what Camillo had been doing, he would not appreciate his son posing as a model. She would never tell him, and if she carried out her intention of leaving, she would have no opportunity to do so. If Cesare needed her, she would stay, but did he? This softened mood would not last, and when he revived, would he turn on her again? But his accusations were without foundation and when she had told him about her meeting with Camillo he would know that he had cruelly misjudged her and they might be able to establish a new relationship, for tonight he had revealed that he desired her and though it was not quite the love for which she longed, it was more than she had thought possible. Out of their union might be born another son to replace the one he had lost.

'I hope Camillo was not in want,' Cesare went on, his mind still occupied by his son. 'That might be why he came back.'

This was Shelagh's cue.

'I assure you he wasn't,' she told him. 'He had a car and he seemed in funds.'

Cesare looked at her as if conscious of her presence for the first time.

'You were in communication with him?' he asked suspiciously.

'Oh no, but I wanted to tell you ...' She knelt down beside him, looking pleadingly up into his face, then she saw he was regarding her with aversion and her words died on her lips.

'I was too hard on him,' he said harshly. 'He knew what you were, didn't he? He found out when he saw you in London. He came back changed, but he lacked the courage to admit he was your dupe. So he ran away. I was the dupe, giving my name to a slut.' He pushed her roughly away.

Shelagh collapsed on the floor at his feet, shrouded by her long hair. She was horrified that he was persisting in his monstrous misconceptions. Dimly she understood that he was trying to justify Camillo's conduct and he could only do so by vilifying herself. The Contessa's poison was still working.

'Now you look like the Magdalene,' Cesare told her. 'She is always depicted with red hair. But I doubt you truly repent.'

Shelagh threw back her hair and rose to her feet. She would make one more effort to make him listen to her.

'Please, Cesare, let me tell you the truth,' she besought him.

'You don't know what truth is,' he said heavily.

Guido materialised from the shadows and looked at her sympathetically. How long he had been listening she did not know.

'*Il maestro* has had a severe shock,' he said to her in a low voice. 'Best leave him to me, *signora*. He is not himself. He will listen to you in the morning.'

'What are you two muttering about?' Cesare rasped. 'Shelagh, go to bed. Guido, pass me the whisky decanter.'

Reluctantly Shelagh went, praying that on the morrow Cesare would be more receptive.

But morning brought Beatrice di Monticelli. Shelagh, who had not slept at all, saw Rita go off to school under Concetta's escort; when it was fine they walked. she had briefly told her that her half-brother had had an accident and her papa was upset.

'Why so?' Rita demanded. 'He didn't like Camillo, neither did I. He's no loss.'

Shelagh rather agreed with her, but told her: 'Please, Rita, he was ... is ... one of the family.'

'Well, I hope he isn't coming back here,' Rita said.

Shelagh warned Concetta not to talk about it. Rita gone, she was standing irresolutely in the hall when the bell rang. Cesare was coming downstairs, looking pale and drawn but quite composed.

'I will see no one,' he declared, and went into the *salotto*.

A manservant opened the door saying, '*Il signor* is not at home.'

The Contessa swept past him. 'He will see me,' she said haughtily. She sailed into the *salotto* and Shelagh followed her.

She went straight up to Cesare and threw her arms round him, and there were real tears in her eyes.

'*Mio amico, mio caro amico,* I have just heard. I came at once.' She spoke in Italian, but Shelagh had no difficulty in following her. 'Such a terrible thing, my heart bleeds for you.' And more extravagant phrases in the same vein. There was no doubt that her concern was perfectly genuine, and Cesare was responding to it. It was what he needed. There were tears in his own eyes as he thanked her brokenly. The Italians are a vociferous and emotional race, and a death is an occasion for drama. Shelagh went quietly out of the room feeling superfluous. Nothing was changed. She would write to the Mother Superior straight away.

CHAPTER TEN

Camillo was interred with all the pomp and circumstance of a Latin funeral. Shelagh found to her great relief that she was not expected to attend, it was a men only ceremony. But she did have to go to the Requiem Mass in the Cathedral, where she nearly fainted amid the clouds of incense, oceans of black crêpe and crocodile tears. A dolorous river of distant relatives, family connections and friends flowed through the villa to offer their condolences. To the Contessa's intense disapproval, Cesare yielded to Shelagh's urging that Rita should board at the convent to escape all this panoply of woe, which would depress her, if nothing worse. The child had never got on with her half-brother, but Beatrice considered her absence showed disrespect for a deceased member of the family. For that was what it was all about. Camillo, the tiresome irresponsible young man, was submerged beneath the homage being paid to the eminent Barsini clan, who had lost the heir to its fortunes.

Shelagh divined that Cesare found comfort in all this ritual, for he seemed to have forgotten Camillo's bad behaviour and blamed himself for abandoning him. She was glad he had not met his son on his return to Genoa. The boy he was mourning was the earlier Camillo who had charmed herself. The brash young man in the red sports car with his American overlay would have offended his family pride. But she had not yet had a chance to exonerate herself, for when Rita went out, Beatrice came in. Her excuse for staying in the house was that Shelagh being a foreigner and unused to Italian protocol could not cope with the influx of visitors. Shelagh did not mind that her place had been usurped, she would not have known what to say to the mournful procession, especially as to her it was all so false.

None of them cared anything about Camillo, and their curiosity about what he had been doing was only thinly disguised. Beatrice was adroit at fending them off, saying Camillo had gone to America because he wanted to see something of that great country before he settled down to the family business. It was such a tragedy that he had died before he had contacted his father, who had eagerly been awaiting his arrival. Shelagh admired her cool self-possession and smooth tongue, wishing she could emulate them, but she did not appreciate the Contessa's monopoly of Cesare. She was always there when he was present in the house, following her own occupations when he was absent at business.

For the first few nights after the accident, Shelagh had lain awake hoping that Cesare would come to her. She intended to receive him with loving submission, and surely when he discovered that she was still a virgin he would admit that he had wronged her. But he never came near her; he took no more notice of her than if she had been a piece of furniture except for the small courtesies of everyday life which were second nature to him. Nor did he repeat his wild accusations, he simply ignored her. Gradually all desire to justify herself died away. It did not much matter, and she did not want to reopen the subject of her relations with Camillo. The Contessa was to all intents and purposes already in her place, and for all she knew Cesare might be visiting her at night; their bedrooms adjoined. That might be why he had lost interest in herself. She waited eagerly for Mother Cecilia's reply to her letter.

But when it came it was not from her but from Sister Joanna, who had always resented her admittance to the convent. Their dearly loved Mother Superior had been called to God. She had become very frail and had died from a sudden attack of pleurisy. Sister Joanna had opened Shelagh's letter as she was dealing with all the deceased's correspondence. Mrs Barsini would be welcome if she would like to spend a few weeks in retreat, but the convent was not a refuge for flighty wives whose right place was beside their husbands, and she hoped Shelagh would think better of leaving hers.

Her one refuge closed to her, Shelagh felt truly bereft, for she had loved the gentle Mother Superior. Amid all the false mourning at the villa, her genuine grief passed unnoticed, and she felt the heavy black she was expected to wear was for Mother Cecilia, not Camillo. Now she would have to make other plans. There seemed no alternative but to go to London and find employment in the field for which she had been trained, but a return to office life was far from alluring.

Rita was chafing at her exile from home, she found the school discipline irksome. Shelagh had promised when she was sent away that she would take her out every weekend. In this Cesare supported her, though Beatrice considered such outings too frivolous during a period of mourning, which infuriated Shelagh. She did not know what Beatrice really thought of Cesare's son, or indeed if she had ever met him, and she flashed out:

'Rita's only a child and I won't have her made miserable. I didn't know you were so attached to Camillo.'

The Contessa looked at her with sad reproachful eyes.

'It is Cesare's grief I respect, which you should do also.'

Shelagh shrugged and said no more. She did not think Cesare had confided in the Contessa his real reason for marrying her, else she would have alluded to it, and for that she was grateful to him.

Rita hated seeing her in black. She knew now that Camillo was dead, but the fact did not distress her.

'Why does everyone have to be so dreary because of Cam?' she kept asking. 'Nobody bothered about him for ages and now all this fuss. *Non capisco.*'

Shelagh reiterated that he had been a Barsini and family, but her tone lacked conviction. She rather agreed with Rita.

Cesare also visited his daughter, and one morning she met him coming out of the school as she was about to go in.

'Ah, Shelagh,' he greeted her. 'I'm so glad you've come. The *piccolina* is moping, and I think it might be a good idea if you and she had a holiday at the Isola di Santa Lucia. You're not looking very well yourself.'

She was surprised he had noticed her appearance, for he never seemed to see her, and though she was longing to leave Genoa, the Isola was the last place she wished to visit, with all its memories of happier days. Moreover she suspected he wanted to get rid of her to be alone with Beatrice.

'Will the Contessa stay at the villa to ... er ... look after you?' she asked sweetly.

'Bea will go back to her own place, of course, and I don't need looking after. I pay my servants to do that.' The grey eyes regarded her quizzically. 'You should be grateful to Bea for carrying out your duties.'

'Oh, I am,' Shelagh said quickly, thinking Beatrice's duties could cover a wide field. 'But I'm surprised you're prepared to send me away with Rita, considering the poor opinion you have of me. Aren't you afraid I'll corrupt her?'

It was the first time either had made any allusion to the night when he had sought to enforce his rights and he looked slightly shamefaced.

'Upon consideration I feel I may have misjudged you,' he told her stiffly.

'You certainly have,' she returned with heat. 'I've never been permissive, Cesare.'

'No, I believe I wronged you there. You were so ... unsophisticated when I first met you, and incapable of deceit. I blame myself, Shelagh, I should have asserted myself. For all your seeming youth, you're a woman, with a woman's needs, so that your lapse was partly my fault.'

'My ... lapse?'

For a moment she did not grasp what he meant, and then a surge of anger swept over her.

'Thank you for your understanding, Cesare, of something that I didn't do,' she blazed. 'How insufferably condescending you are, and such a hypocrite! All this parade of grief for Cam. My God, if you'd seen what he'd turned into you'd have had a shock!'

His hand shot out and gripped her wrist.

'You saw him?'

'I did. It was he I met that afternoon when you saw someone kiss me.'

His lip curled with distaste. 'Your stepson?'

'Yes. We'd just realised our relationship, so he kissed his *matrigna,* as he called me. Do you mind that? You people are always kissing each other.'

'You never told me.'

'I tried to, but you wouldn't listen. Lately I haven't had a chance to speak to you. Your mistress was always in the way.'

His grip tightened on her wrist until she thought the bones would crack. 'How dare you refer to the Contessa as my mistress!'

Shelagh's eyes sparkled like green gems in her pale face.

'Isn't she?'

'Certainly not. I respect Bea.'

'But you don't respect me. Cesare, you're hurting me!'

He looked down at her fragile wrist with a cruel little smile curving his lips. Cesare ... Borgia, she thought. He has the wrong surname.

'I'll end by hurting more than your wrist, you maddening little devil,' he said harshly.

'Thank you for those few kind words.'

'Váttene!' He dropped her wrist which felt numb. 'You'll tell Rita about going to Venezia?'

'But I haven't said I'll go.'

He smiled crookedly. 'You'll go, if only to get away from me. *Ciao*, Shelagh.'

He was gone, striding rapidly towards his car.

Shelagh watched his receding figure, absently rubbing her maltreated wrist. She was regretting her quick temper. Not thus had she meant to reveal that Camillo had been her supposed lover and all he had wanted was to be reconciled to his father. His preliminary love talk had meant nothing, being completely phoney, Camillo's way of trying to soften her. She should not have referred to Beatrice as Cesare's mistress, which, though it might possibly be true, was certain to annoy him. Well-bred Italian wives were supposed to wink at such irregularities. All she had achieved from her mishandling of the situation was a bruised wrist and the appellation 'maddening little devil'. With a sigh she turned to enter the school, resolving that she would acquaint Cesare with her intention of returning to England that night.

Shelagh took Rita to lunch at an inexpensive *trattoria* where she knew the food would not be too elaborate. Cesare continued to pay her a large allowance and she would have plenty in hand for her ticket to London. As soon as she was earning again she would repay it.

Rita chattered away gaily about her teachers and her friends. She was at the age when schoolgirls in segregated establishments develop 'pashes' for older women and girls. Her present idol was a young nun who taught divinity.

'She has a face like a saint,' Rita declared, 'and she never gets angry with us. Not all the Sisters are saint-like, they seem to become a bit sour when they've been there a long time.'

'I'm not surprised, having to cope with imps like you,' Shelagh said, laughing.

'Oh, but I'm very, very good at school,' Rita protested. 'But I'd hate to have to enter an Order. Zia Beatrice says Mamma was half a saint, which is why God called her away so soon. Perhaps that's why Papa didn't like her very much.'

'Rita, what a thing to say!' Shelagh expostulated. 'Whatever gave you that idea?' It was the reverse of what Beatrice said.

'Well, he never talks about her, and he doesn't keep any photos of her, and everyone except Aunt Bea knows he married her for her money. It'll be mine when I'm grown up, and I shall spend it all quickly so my husband will love me for myself alone. You didn't have any money, did you, Mamma?'

'No, I didn't,' Shelagh said bleakly.

'Then of course Papa married *you* for love.'

How wrong can you get? Shelagh thought. Rita

seemed to have forgotten that she had been engaged to Camillo. The child went on:

'You're so pretty and your hair's gorgeous. Zia Bea says red hair is common, but that's not right. All the best Venetians have red-gold hair. There's a poem we've read in class, something about...

"Dear, dead women, with such hair too—What's become of all the gold?—
Used to hang and brush their bosoms."

I think it's super. It's about Venice, of course.'

'I'm surprised the Sisters let you read Browning,' Shelagh said, a little embarrassed by this flattery. 'But you're rather young, darling, to be thinking about love and marriage.'

'It's all the bigger girls talk about when the nuns aren't listening.'

Shelagh glanced sadly at the heart-shaped face within its frame of dark curls. Rita had her father's good looks and the passionate Italian temperament. Would the Contessa be a sympathetic guide through the jungle of adolescent emotions? She doubted it, but she could not stay for Rita's sake, for her influence would be constantly undermined by the other woman, who had a greater knowledge of what Cesare would expect from his daughter than she, the alien, could ever instil into her.

She came home after an afternoon in the cinema and taking Rita back to school to find an extraordinary difference in the atmosphere. For the first time since Camillo's funeral, all the blinds were up and some of the windows were open. The Contessa had persisted in keeping the house shrouded in gloom. It had been a mild day with a promise of spring in the air. Mimosa was coming into flower in sheltered places and the sea was a vivid blue reflecting a cloudless sky.

Some of the maids were actually singing in the kitchen regions. Concetta was in her room when Shelagh reached it. Since Rita had gone she had taken to maiding her mistress, fearful perhaps of being found redundant and she was going through the wardrobe.

'What will the Signora wear for dinner?' she asked. 'The Signore has said he will be in.'

Good, Shelagh thought. I'll get him alone afterwards and tell him I want to go away. Though want was hardly the right word. When she left she would leave her heart behind her.

'The black thing, of course,' she said. She had bought a thin black dress for evening wear with a high neck and sleeves.

'I thought perhaps the Signora might prefer a white dress for a change,' Concetta suggested diffidently. 'Is not like wearing colours, and the Signora looks so lovely in white.'

Shelagh smiled ruefully; she was heartily tired of the black dress.

'Thank you, Concetta, but the Contessa would throw a fit if I appeared in anything but black.'

'The Contessa has gone to her own home.'

Shelagh stared at her in surprise. 'Really?'

The maid giggled. 'The *maestro* came home for *collazione*, and they argued. Then she told Guido to call a taxi and packed her bags. When she had gone we rolled all the blinds up.'

'So I saw,' Shelagh commented. 'The Contessa doesn't seem to be very popular with the staff.'

Concetta shrugged. 'Is old-fashioned. Then you will wear the white, *signora*?'

Shelagh said she would. It seemed too good to be true that Beatrice had departed. Possibly after her taunt, Cesare had realised that her continued presence in his house was giving rise to gossip. Then she remembered that she had been ordered to take Rita to the Isola, he seemed certain she would go. Coming back from her bath, she saw that Concetta had laid out the classical gown she had worn at her first dinner party. About to look for something simpler, she changed her mind. This would be her last opportunity to wear it, for she intended to leave the bulk of her extensive wardrobe behind her for Cesare to dispose of as he pleased; the garments were more his than hers. Her summer tan had finally faded and she was a symphony in white and gold with the long flowing skirt falling to her feet. She wore no jewellery except an enamelled locket that had belonged to her before either of the Barsinis had entered her orbit. Jewels would have no place in her future. The emeralds were of course in Cesare's safe. She wondered if he would give them to Beatrice or keep them for Margarita. If they had been her mother's as she suspected they should go to the child.

A spasm of pain crossed her face as she recalled how Cesare had said they matched her eyes on that far-distant evening when he had put them about her neck to impress Gillian. He had been so kind and thoughtful ... then. Gillian would have decamped with anything she could collect, but ... she was not Gillian. Perhaps she was sensitive and unmercenary to the point of foolishness, but she could not change her nature. Then she noticed her discoloured wrist, and covered it with the diamond bracelet Cesare had given her at Christmas. Perhaps she would keep that as recompense for his brutal behaviour.

Cesare did not appear until the gong sounded for dinner—a piece of old-fashioned ceremony he insisted upon. He was wearing a dark blue velvet coat, what used to be called a smoking jacket instead of the formal black and white he had put on every night while Beatrice was staying with them. The general relaxation since her departure seemed to have spread to him.

Their conversation was a little stilted over dinner while the servants waited upon them. Both were recalling the words spoken outside the convent that afternoon. Beatrice was still between them, though not bodily present. Cesare asked her how she and Rita had spent their time and Shelagh described the lush but innocuous Italian picture they had seen. The photography had been good but the content too appallingly sentimental.

'Still, she seemed to enjoy it,' she concluded.

'You've no use for sentimentality?'

'No, it's false. I hate any sort of artifice and insincerity.'

'Quite so,' he said drily, and she blushed, remembering that she had called him a hypocrite. She wished he did not look so devastatingly attractive. The lines of strain and fatigue had gone from his smooth olive face, and his grey eyes held a mocking glint. She wondered what was in his mind behind his unrevealing expression. She noticed there was more silver at his temples than when she had first known him, it made him look even more distinguished. Her eyes travelled over the polished table with its lace mats, silver and Venetian glasses; the handsome épergne holding a bowl of fruit. She was going to miss all this, and more, much more, the presence of its autocratic owner who had always been something of an enigma to her.

'Shall we have coffee in the *salotto*?' he asked when the meal was concluded.

'Please.'

She walked before him into the sitting room, surprised that he seemed disposed to honour her with his company. Until Beatrice's advent, he had usually gone out. He turned on the television for the news and made several remarks about current events. The maid brought in the coffee tray and placed it in front of Shelagh.

'Please turn that thing off, Cesare,' she said sharply, nervousness making her abrupt. 'I want to talk to you.'

'*Bene, mia cara.*' He switched off the machine and taking his coffee cup sat down in an easy chair opposite to her, crossing his long legs. 'Go ahead.'

She hesitated, fiddling with her coffee spoon, seeking for the right words. Finally she said simply:

'I want to go away.'

'I suggested that this afternoon. Venezia awaits you.'

'No, Cesare, I mean I want to go for good, back to England and get a job.'

He gave her one of his steely looks. 'Why?'

'Oh,' she cried passionately, 'it's obvious, isn't it? Our marriage is a farce. You don't trust me and the Contessa is the real mistress of this house. It would be much better to end it all so that she can take her rightful place.'

Again she was expressing herself badly. She had not meant to mention Beatrice, but her burning resentment of the woman had found voice.

Cesare was looking at her steadily and when he spoke his voice was very cold.

'Will you ever grow up, Shelagh? The truth is you are piqued because Bea has managed a difficult situation with which you were unable to cope yourself: You seem to have become obsessed with the poor woman to the extent that you want to run away. Understand, if you go rushing off to England, I shall not come to fetch you back.'

'I wouldn't expect you to.' Angry colour flooded her cheeks and her eyes were green fire. 'I'm serious, Cesare, I want this to be final. It isn't only the Contessa, it's everything. I ... I'm not the right wife for you, in fact I never have been a wife. You married me to ... to save my face. It was very noble of you and I'm grateful, but it was a mistake.' She suddenly became calm, her colour ebbing. 'I propose to go back to my old life. I don't suppose you'll have much difficulty in getting an annulment since we haven't ... you know what I mean. I shall leave at once.'

'And if I refuse to let you go?'

She cried out in panic, 'You can't keep me here against my will!'

'Perhaps not.' He was smiling. 'But I could break your will.'

'What do you mean?' she asked faintly, suddenly afraid. 'You wouldn't lock me up?'

'An intriguing suggestion, but mediaeval. Still, some of those ancient practices could be used with advantage on the present generation, such as the shrew's bridle and the chastity belt—effective if uncomfortable.' His eyes were gleaming wickedly, and Shelagh's temper flared.

'Damn you, Cesare, be serious! It may please your perverted sense of humour to talk such rubbish, but you know I've made a most practical suggestion. We'd be better apart.'

'There I disagree with you, my little spitfire.' He rose from his chair and coming across to her pulled her up into his arms. 'You're most provoking when you're angry, I can't resist the challenge. You know what your trouble is, you're eaten up with jealousy of poor Bea and your grievance is that I haven't slept with you. *Bene*, that can be easily remedied.'

'No, Cesare, please,' she cried wildly. 'That won't solve anything.' She tried to fight free of his arms. 'You don't love me.'

'Don't I?'

She became suddenly still. 'How ... how could you?'

'It is rather surprising, isn't it? Especially as I doubt my feelings are returned.' He released his hold and let her slip back into her chair, then balanced himself on the edge of a table at a little distance from her. 'Listen, *mia cara,* I want to tell you a little story. Once upon a time a certain simple maiden left her native land to marry a young prince. She had red-gold hair, green eyes and a skin like milk. But the prince had a spell laid upon him by a wicked enchantress who wafted him away to the other side of the world, and our poor little heroine found herself alone in a foreign country with no one to succour her.'

'But I know all that,' Shelagh said fretfully, wondering what he was getting at.

'Not quite all. *Bene,* came a black knight in the best tradition to the rescue of the poor deserted one. She seemed to him so fragile and appealing in her distress he wondered how the prince *could* have left her. The only solution for her plight was to marry her himself. But he did not presume to imagine that she, so young and fair, could fancy a tough old widower as he was, but he had hope, and he waited.' He paused, then went on with a throb of deep feeling in his voice. 'Yes, Shelagh, I waited. I strove to fulfil all your wishes, I gave you what I had to give, but you remained cool and aloof, an ice maiden. You looked upon me as an indulgent father when I wanted a loving wife. It seemed that I was too old, too set in my ways to touch your little hard heart. Do you wonder that I found Bea's friendship more rewarding? Not that it has ever been more than friendship. Then I saw you in the street, embracing a young man, and I believed that that was the secret of your coldness to me. You had a young lover whom you met when I was conveniently absent, for I never attempted to curtail your liberty.—

No, let me finish,' as Shelagh tried to speak. 'I should of course have given you a chance to explain, but I'm only human. I went mad, I saw red, I meant to take what you would not give me. But you know what happened.' His gaze held hers with a fixed intensity. 'The prince had returned, and finding his loved one faithless ... *killed himself*.'

'Oh!' Shelagh sprang to her feet, her eyes blazing. 'You know that that's a wicked lie!'

'Is it? You've confessed that it was Camillo you met, Camillo whom you had loved so much. You had to tell him that you were beyond his reach, his stepmother in fact. Weren't you both heartbroken at the irony of fate?'

'Not in the least,' Shelagh returned promptly. 'I found I didn't even like him, and as for him, he only wanted to use me to get in touch with you. Cam was quite incapable of killing himself for any woman, the only person he loved was himself. I'm sorry now that I refused to help him, but I ... I didn't want to see him again, and I don't wonder he had a smash—he drove like a maniac.'

'Thank you,' Cesare said gravely. 'I merely wanted to be sure of your reaction to him. I presume that is the truth?'

'Of course it is. And since you're so sceptical, I'll give you the whole truth, though I doubt you'll believe it. What I felt for Cam wasn't love. I've only had one love, and that's yourself. I ... I didn't want to love you, but it's happened, and now I'm stuck with it. I shall never love anyone else.'

'But being a cold little English iceberg, you concealed this great love under a mountain of snow?'

'Oh, don't mock me!' she cried despairingly. She turned away with a half sob. 'I have some pride, and you didn't want me.'

'Want you!' he exclaimed with sudden passion. He took her by her shoulders and turned her to face him. 'I know all about Camillo and what happened. I made enquiries and one of the persons interrogated was the waitress at the *caffé* where you had tea, an old flame of his, incidentally, But it hurt me that you could not bring yourself to confide in me.'

'How could I, with the Contessa always here? I never saw you alone.'

'I was alone at night in my room,' he pointed out. 'As my wife you had access to it, or did you think you'd find Bea there?' Shelagh blushed and hung her head. 'For shame, Shelagh, but I'll admit Bea did presume too much. I told her I would never take a fourth wife, it would be ludicrous, I'm not a film star, but being a woman she was persistent.'

'You're a much married man,' Shelagh observed mischievously.

'But I've never really had a wife. Maria died when I was twenty, and Carlotta was always ill. At least I know you're healthy.' His eyes fell on the bracelet on her wrist. He pushed it up to disclose the purple bruise and he looked shocked. 'Did I do that? I was a brute, but continual frustration made me cruel.' He bent his head swiftly and set his lips on it.

Looking down on his dark head, Shelagh asked:

'Why on earth did you suggest that Cam killed himself?'

He glanced at her, grinning. 'To shock you into telling the truth. I got a better response than I hoped for.'

'Oh, you devious Italian!' Shelagh cried. 'And now I've given myself away, where do we go from here?'

'Where do you suppose? Upstairs, of course.'

She blushed again and he became serious. 'You've a lot to forgive, *mia cara*, can you be magnanimous?'

'Oh, Cesare, I'd forgive you anything!'

He looked down at her with laughter in his eyes.

'Even if I told you I'd made love to Bea?'

'Well ... er ...' Her expression was dubious.

'I swear to you I never have.' He drew her into his arms. 'You are the love of my life, Shelagh. Do you still want to go to England?'

'No, but I would like a holiday on the Isola, if you'll come too.'

'Do you think I'd let you go without me ... now?'

His hold tightened and his mouth came down on hers.

Later he lifted her in his arms and carried her up the marble staircase, along the corridor and into her white and gold room, with the wide imperial bed. Outside in the velvet Italian night someone was singing on the terrace next door *Amore mia,* accompanied by a mandolin.

LEO

Harlequin Horoscope

YOUR LOVE-NATURE

EARTH SIGN July 23-August 22

Your Leo love-nature is warm, romantic, idealistic and loyal. Leo is the sign that rules the heart; so, not surprisingly, "affairs of the heart" are very important to you. Pride and high self-esteem are among your major characteristics; you are never happy without the admiration and respect of the people around you. But you really glow only when there is one special person whose dependable, devoted love envelops you with warmth.

One of your most charming characteristics is that you idealize the one you love, attributing all sorts of good qualities to him. This tends to bring out the best in your lover, who tries to live up to your high opinion. You will make any sacrifice for love and in fact are romantic enough to welcome obstacles, which you can then overcome to show your devotion. Unfortunately this attitude sometimes leads you astray. A person who needs you appeals to your chivalrous instincts, and thus you tend to become involved, only to find that this person is not worthy of your idealism and loyalty. For this reason Leo is often disappointed in love.

As partners, the other fire signs, Aries and Sagittarius, are very good because they share your idealism and warmth. Another Leo might also suit you, but you both love being noticed and admired, so there would be constant competition for the spotlight. The cooler air signs—Libra, Aquarius and Gemini—enjoy your buoyancy and friendliness, and would probably be content to let you be the "star" as long as they were having fun, too.